LORDS OF HAVESHAM MANOR, VOLUME 3

Graham's Game
Victor's Vow

Josie Dennis

MENAGE AMOUR

Siren Publishing, Inc.
www.SirenPublishing.com

A SIREN PUBLISHING BOOK
IMPRINT: Ménage Amour

LORDS OF HAWKSFELL MANOR, VOLUME 3
Graham's Game
Victor's Vow

Copyright © 2014 by Josie Dennis

ISBN: 978-1-62740-760-1

First Printing: February 2014

Graham's Game
Victor's Vow
    Cover design © Harris Channing
Print cover design by Siren-BookStrand
All cover art and logo copyright © 2014 by Siren Publishing, Inc.

Printed in the U.S.A.

PUBLISHER
Siren Publishing, Inc.
www.SirenPublishing.com

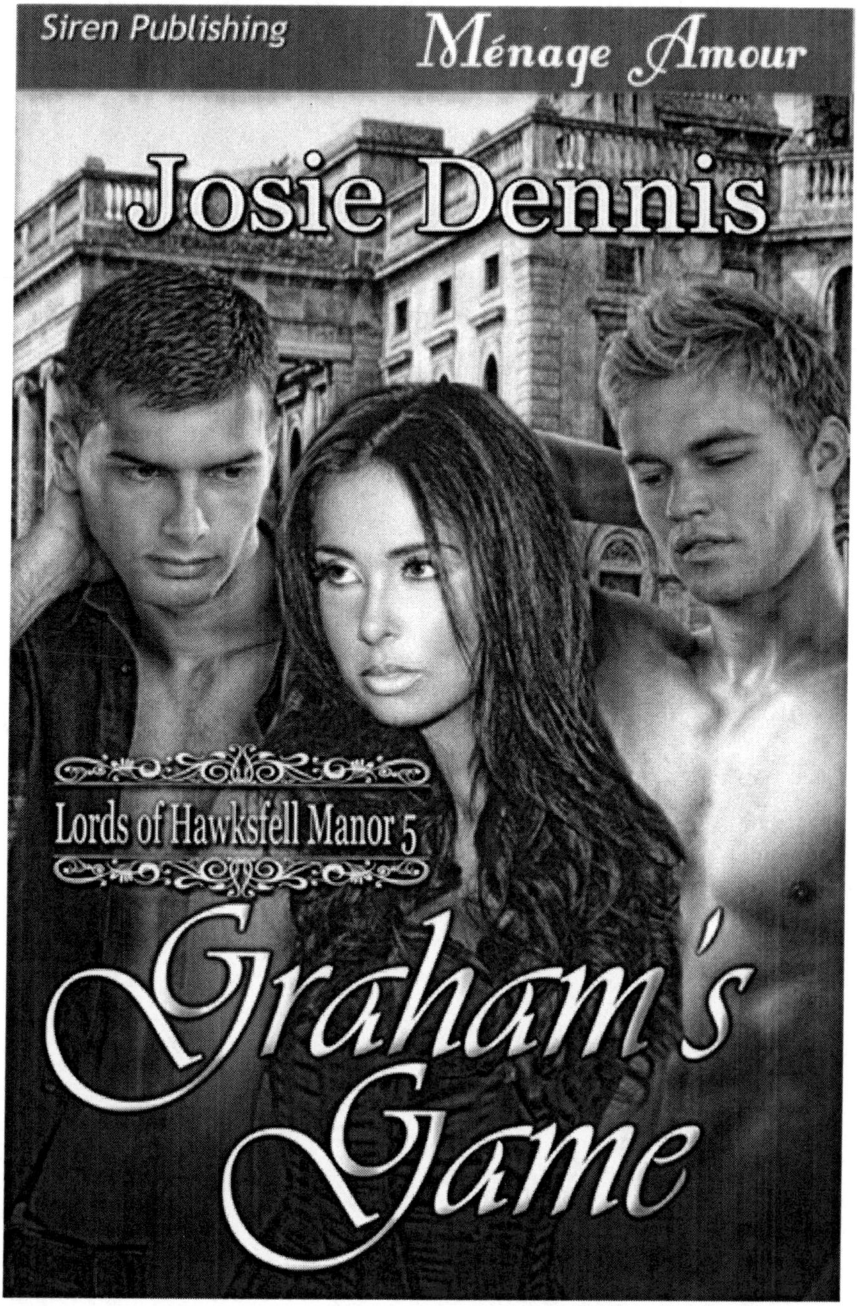
Siren Publishing
Ménage Amour
Josie Dennis
Lords of Hawksfell Manor 5
Graham's Game

GRAHAM'S GAME

Lords of Hawksfell Manor 5

JOSIE DENNIS
Copyright © 2014

Chapter 1

Yorkshire, England 1912

Graham Hawk, Viscount Weston, collapsed on the bed, his breath still coming fast. "That was quite a ride!" He'd fucked forever, wringing every drop of pleasure out of tonight's woman.

His best friend Colin Spencer let out a grunt of satisfaction and nodded his dark head. "Too right."

The woman sprawled between them murmured some soft sounds and cuddled against Graham's flat belly, her long blond hair draped over his chest. He absently stroked her back, feeling that familiar sense of detachment that always followed his orgasm. His beast was sated and his cursed Hawk lust under control. It was always this way, and it was how he preferred it.

He and Colin had each ridden her hard, taking turns in her pussy before letting her suck them both off. They were in exact accord tonight, as they usually were. Their lusts were matched, astounding as that should be. From when they first met at Cambridge, he'd found that Colin was nearly as insatiable as he was. That fact made these pussy raids more enjoyable for Graham over the years. He might be cursed with his Hawk lusts, but it was nice to have a friend with him when the urge rose. If nothing else, it saved him any regret or guilt he might feel for succumbing otherwise.

Guilt. Why the hell should he feel guilty? He gave as much pleasure as he took. He was a Hawk, after all. He could fuck forever. Pussy, mouth, ass, it didn't matter.

"Money's on the table, my girl," Colin said, giving her ass a smack.

She giggled and climbed over them to stand beside the bed. Graham watched as her eyes roamed over his and Colin's bodies. They were both tall men, though Colin's body was more beautiful than his own, smoothly muscled and very fit. Graham was burlier but quite proud of his size, and not just the length and breadth of his fine Hawk cock. By the light in the girl's eyes he knew they'd both pleased her, though she obviously wouldn't be averse to another ride and soon.

He watched as she donned her slip and gathered up her quickly discarded dress. She picked up the money then hesitated, turning toward them again.

"Good night, love." Graham sat up and brushed his sun-streaked hair off his forehead. "Perhaps Mr. Spencer and I will call upon you again."

Her eyes flared, and she nodded. She left them then, closing the door tight behind her. Colin chuckled and Graham arched a brow at him.

"You shouldn't give the girl false hope, Graham."

Graham shrugged. "I might not ever take the same lover twice, but you might want to fuck her again."

"Not without you." Colin stilled then grinned. "I'm sure she'd miss your attentions."

Something had passed over his friend's face in that brief moment, a hesitation of some sort. But if Colin could set it aside, so could Graham.

"You're nearly as randy as my fine self, Colin. I'm sure you could handle her alone."

Colin dipped his head in agreement. "Are you off to Weston Park, then?"

Graham stood and pulled on his trousers. "Where else?"

Colin didn't say a word but starting dressing himself. Graham knew what he was thinking, though. Colin was quite wealthy and had access to several properties despite his lack of title. One of his houses was just up the road from the pleasing little Inn at Helmsley. In fact, Graham had spent the past week in his company there. As for Graham, for his Hawk legitimacy and his Weston title, he had only his mother's aunt and uncle's house to call home. His father had left an estate in his name here in Yorkshire and it paid handsomely every quarter, but he'd never even set eyes on it.

"Come stay with me for a while longer," Colin said, shrugging into his jacket. "Never say you have any pressing engagements at Weston Park."

Graham straightened his own clothes then shook his head. "A short ride on a brisk November evening would be very pleasant, but I don't want to impose on your hospitality any longer."

Colin smiled, that familiar expression that made him look very much like the young easygoing man he truly was. Though they were both barely twenty-seven, Graham found he always had to work to appear as carefree as Colin.

"Impose?" Colin asked. "After what we both shared?"

"Are you offering your staff to me?" Graham asked with a smile. "Haven't I fucked them already?"

Colin winked. "Mostly."

Graham shook his head. "Thank you, but no."

"Why not?"

He couldn't voice his reasons, but he had to be alone. Well, relatively alone. His great aunt and uncle never had much to do with him, and now that they were firmly in their dotage they had even less.

Colin nodded, but his blue eyes were a little clouded. Graham felt that familiar pull toward him and a chill of fear washed over him. He plastered on his usual playful grin.

"I'll see you within a fortnight," Graham said.

He left the room and went down to call for his motor. It was tempting to stay with Colin at Spencer House. He'd never felt closer to another person in his entire life, and he doubted he ever would. He really couldn't afford that attachment, though. It was dangerous to depend on another person for your happiness.

To him, life was a game he played by his own rules. He presented a jovial face to the world and kept his wants and needs to himself, save for the sexual ones. Those he indulged with abandon and had since gaining manhood.

His great uncle had told him a bit about the curse that dogged all of the Hawks, and Graham had scoffed until the first time he'd attempted to ease himself with his hand. It proved impossible. Orgasm was followed swiftly by stabbing pains in his belly and a burgeoning erection that lasted for hours. From then on, he fucked the Weston Park staff, fellow students at Cambridge, or serving maids at accommodating country inns. Aside from pussy raids with Colin, he withdrew in solitude afterward. If he felt lonely or empty after release, he didn't need any of his lovers to know that. That was the reason he never took the same lover twice. Familiarity would disclose him for the fraud he was.

He and Colin had pleasured each other when they shared women, but he didn't count that as a tryst. Colin was his friend. His only friend, if he were being honest with himself. But after spending a week with him, he had to withdraw again.

It wouldn't do to foster an attachment that wouldn't last. And if he'd learned anything from his parents' desertion, it was that Hawks didn't do forever.

* * * *

Lily D'ursey arranged the pretty bottles and silver hair combs and brushes on the delicately-carved vanity. Her job as lady's maid to the Countess of Hawksfell was fulfilling and a better position than she dared to hope for when she found herself unemployed in London three months ago. After an unfortunate and abrupt dismissal from her previous position, she'd been thrilled to overhear the countess's cousin say that they needed to find temporary help while in town. That led to this permanent position, once she convinced the old baron to write her the glowing recommendation she deserved. It was the least the old letch could do after that last horrid night she'd spent under his roof.

The countess was beautiful and kind, and quite undemanding. In fact, she truly didn't like to be fussed over. As a result Lily was often at sixes and sevens, with nothing more to occupy her than her mistress's mending. She was content though, and at twenty-two years old, she hoped this position would last for a good many years.

The servants downstairs were friendly enough, but as a lady's maid she was a bit above their level. She had no friends among the staff, most of whom had worked for the earl for years. She'd thought at first that she could get close to one of the parlormaids, Posy, but amazingly that girl had recently married the earl's half-brother of all people. Imagine, a maid marrying above her station and gaining a husband who clearly loved her!

"Are you still playing about with the countess's fripperies, Lily?" Cabot asked from the doorway.

She took a breath and turned to face the footman. "I am doing my work, Cabot. Never say you're checking on me."

Cabot flashed his most charming smile. "I *might* say I am."

Lily eyed him. The blond young man was tall and handsome, as a good footman should be. He'd been after her for weeks now, but she was less than interested.

"I'll not have any of that funny business, Cabot."

He shook his head, his blue eyes bright. "Just because you couldn't catch Mosley, don't be prickly, love."

"What cheek!" She stiffened, her heart racing at what he insinuated. "I wasn't trying to catch Mosley. And don't call me love!"

Sailing past him, she left her lady's room and hurried down the hall toward the back stairs. Cabot was pretty to look at, but he was too glib by half. She *had* been interested in Mosley, the earl's chauffeur who now worked for one of the earl's Hawk relatives. And was romantically involved with him too, if her suspicions were correct.

She knew men could love men. That didn't surprise her. In fact, one of the old baron's footmen was deeply in love with an under-gardener. It certainly wouldn't be the first time a Hawk had taken up with one or more of the earl's staff, either. Why, even the earl's half-brother was involved with William, the first footman, as well his wife, the former parlormaid Posy! It was passing strange that they could love two people, but she believed it had something to do with the Hawk curse.

She'd heard whispers about it in her time here at the manor, but she'd been unable to get at the particulars. It wasn't her business really, but all of the Hawks were just so compelling. They all had the earl's dark eyes, handsome face, and muscular build. It was little wonder the women in their lives had succumbed. Of course, those women *wanted* sensual involvement. Lily most certainly did not, her passing infatuation with Mosley the chauffeur notwithstanding. That part of her life was over before it began, thanks to the old baron.

"Not for me, thank you very much," she told herself as she stepped down into the servants' hall.

"What's that, Lily?" Mrs. Holmes asked.

Lily straightened her spine. She clasped her hands and nodded to the housekeeper. "Nothing at all, Mrs. Holmes."

It was said the housekeeper all but raised the earl from a babe and felt a strong connection to all the Hawks. There was little the she missed. The older woman tilted her graying head, her eyes sharp. Then she gave Lily a small smile and went past her toward the stairs.

Lily watched her go. For a second she'd longed to ask her about the Hawk curse. It was shrouded with talk of dark, delicious desires and earthy sensuality. She was sure of it. All of the Hawks radiated strong sexual magnetism. There was something about a beast that rose and demanded satisfaction, as well. In spite of herself, her body began to tingle.

"Almost time for dinner service," one of the other footmen said as he rushed past her toward the kitchen.

She wasn't needed to serve, so she poured herself a cup of tea and settled in the common room. She sat at the long table with a book, blocking out the sounds of the kitchen staff just across the way. The family would eat upstairs, and afterwards the staff would eat down here. It was how things were done, and Lily liked the routine. It was comfortable dining with the others and Mrs. Holmes. It almost felt like family.

She wouldn't think about what always came after, when she was alone in her attic room with nothing to occupy her mind but loneliness. She was nothing like the countess, sweet and beautiful. Or even like Posy, bubbly and pretty. She couldn't entertain any thoughts of love or true connection, not with a Hawk or a servant.

She would live her very comfortable life alone and be happy for it. It was no hardship, really. Indeed, it was a small price to pay for her safety.

Chapter 2

Colin sat at his dining table, alone as usual. His heart thudded in his chest as he thought of that last night with Graham over a week ago. He'd left him. Again. They'd shared a girl as they'd done many times before, but it had seemed like more than that that night. Graham had stayed with him here at his country house and Colin had begun to hope they could deepen their friendship at last.

He was growing tired of keeping his feelings inside and only playing by Graham's rules. He hadn't said anything that night, though. He wouldn't say anything the next time he saw him, either. The last thing he wanted was to make his best friend uncomfortable.

They'd been close from the first. And from the first, Colin had sensed something inside Graham. He needed connection even though he often professed the opposite. The atmosphere at Weston Park fed that illusion. His great aunt and uncle were pleased to continue their quiet life, now that the boy they'd welcomed into their home as a baby was an independent adult. Graham came and went as he chose, and Colin was grateful he was the companion he preferred.

As for Colin, his family was loud and numbered many, but at his country house in Yorkshire he found the solitude he sometimes needed. Graham was the only person he ever invited to stay, even for the shortest time. There had been lovers during his long association with Graham, women who held his attention for some time or other before he grew bored. Where Graham never took the same lover twice, it was Colin's secret wish to find the person who could hold his attention—and his heart—for longer than a fortnight. Aside from Graham, there really hadn't been anyone whose company he craved for any length of time.

"Not so different from Graham there," he muttered.

He finished eating and left the room. A quiet evening spent in front of the fire seemed to be in the offing. The wind buffeted the tall, leaded windows of the parlor. He shuddered at the sound. It seemed to enhance his loneliness tonight. He poured himself a glass of brandy and took a long sip. The liquor burned pleasantly down his throat and warmed his belly. Closing his eyes, he let his head fall against the back of the chair. A knock at the door brought him out of his melancholy.

"Come," he said without much enthusiasm.

His butler opened the door and bowed. "Lord Weston, sir."

Colin straightened as Graham strode into the room. His hair was windswept and his cheeks ruddy, but it was the wide smile on his face that took Colin aback. It was fresh and wild and full of excitement. He hadn't seen such an expression on Graham's face in ages.

"Graham!" He stood, setting his drink down on the table beside the chair. "I wasn't expecting you."

"Never say you're turning me back out into the cold."

Colin laughed. "Hardly." He crossed to doorway and shook his hand. "Not expecting you doesn't mean I'm not pleased to see you."

Graham nodded and removed his coat. The butler took it and looked at Colin for instruction.

"Prepare Lord Weston's usual guest room, Mason."

The butler bowed his head and left them, closing the door behind him. Colin poured a drink for Graham and held out the glass. "Do tell me what has you rapping on my door in the dead of night."

Graham laughed, flicking his golden-streaked hair back from his face. His dark Hawk eyes sparkled. "I have been invited to the infamous Hawk roost, Colin."

Colin blinked. "Hawksfell Manor?"

Graham arched a brow. "You've heard of it?"

"It's infamous, Graham. You just said so yourself."

"So I did." He shrugged and settled into the chair Colin had just vacated. "The esteemed earl's man-of-affairs sent me a missive extending an invitation from the man himself."

Colin sat across from him. "Why?"

"Apparently the earl has dedicated himself to saving wayward Hawks." He laughed. "His man tracked me down, no doubt due to my scandalous behavior."

Colin leveled a look at him. "Scandalous to a Hawk? Not if half of what I've heard of your extended family is true."

"All is true, I'm afraid." Graham winked. "You've seen me firsthand, Colin. At my worst."

There was a thread of something beneath Graham's teasing tone. Was it regret or embarrassment? Colin didn't believe so.

"When is this auspicious visit?" he asked Graham.

"I responded that the earl is to expect me in two days' time."

"I'm sure you'll have a fine time getting to know the earl and his family."

"His family?"

"Do you truly not know?"

"Know what?"

"The earl married over the summer. There are a few Hawk cousins about now, as well. Along with a half-brother he hadn't known he'd had."

A frown passed over Graham's face. "He has a family."

"As do you, if you think about it. You're a Hawk."

"Yes, yes." Graham nodded absently. "Maybe I should reconsider."

"Why?"

"I thought this would be a lark, Colin. I'd heard about the earl's staff, paid to serve his dark desires with enthusiasm and discretion."

Colin nodded. "I'd heard that, too. For years, actually."

"Then it's true." He smiled again. "Then we must take the earl up on his offer and play a few games with his staff."

Colin grew quiet for a moment. "If you wish," he finally said.

Graham tilted his head. "Come now, Colin. Never say you're not up to a bit of fun."

Colin found a smile. "With you? Always."

Something flared in Graham's eyes, a heat that Colin felt echoed in his belly. Desire was clear on his handsome face, that need that was never silent for long. His Hawk lust was rising, and Colin couldn't help but respond.

"I've missed you, Colin," Graham said, surprising him. "It's deuced quiet at Weston."

Colin didn't point out that he'd invited him to stay here just last week. They both knew it. He'd thought Graham would want to fuck one of the maids again, but the expression he wore said something more. Something elemental that Colin couldn't deny.

"When do you leave for Hawksfell Manor?" he asked, his voice low.

Graham reached out and stroked a strong hand over Colin's thigh. "When do *we* leave, you mean?" At Colin's nod, he smiled. "Tomorrow would suffice."

Colin swallowed thickly. "I'll be ready."

Graham's eyes ran over him, and Colin couldn't keep himself from reacting. "Ready?" His low laugh was like a caress. "Oh, I hope so."

Colin stood, unable and unwilling to disguise the erection tenting his trousers. "Shall I ring for a maid?"

"Not yet." Graham stepped closer. "Maybe later."

"A footman, then?"

Graham shook his head and brought his mouth to his. "Just kiss me, Colin."

They'd never kissed. Not once. Colin pressed his lips to Graham and tasted him. He sucked on his tongue and caught Graham's groan. His hands were firm on Colin's ass, and he felt Graham's long hard cock against his belly. Yes, they'd pleased each other before but they had never shared only each other's company.

Colin pulled back, his heart racing as he read the desire on Graham's face again. "Upstairs?" he managed to ask.

Graham smiled.

* * * *

Graham followed Colin up the grand staircase to his rooms. His country house was really quite comfortable, and Graham had spent many pleasant nights under its well-maintained roof. But tonight felt different. He had to come here tonight, after passing too many lonely days at Weston Park. He'd been seized with the need to see his friend.

Though he'd asked for it, Colin's kiss had been a surprise. It was sweet and hot, just like his best friend. His cock pounded in his trousers, and he doubted they would need to add some servant to the mix tonight. No. Tonight he wanted Colin.

His stay at Weston Park had been beyond dull. His great aunt and uncle were as quiet as the grave, bringing to mind the inevitability of their leaving him as his parents had. Truth was, he didn't even know if his mother and father were still alive. It felt strange to consider being truly alone in the world.

Colin stopped in front of his door and arched a dark brow. Graham needed him tonight, and not just because his cursed Hawk cock was hard and ready. He wanted a connection along with release, and who better to find that with than his best friend?

"Proceed," Graham urged. "I fear I'm about to split my trouser seams."

Colin smiled, losing that apparent doubt Graham had glimpsed in his blue eyes. In fact, he seemed as ready to go as Graham was himself. They disrobed and again Graham was struck by Colin's masculine beauty. He'd had men before, in their mouths or their asses, but it had been for a quick release. At the back of his mind a thought teased him. This felt like more, and he couldn't have that.

This was what it was, and he would take what Colin wanted to give and please him in return.

He shed his clothes, letting them drop to the floor. His cock was hard and throbbing now, his every muscle tense. Colin hissed in a breath, and Graham met his eyes. They burned hot, an electric blue flame. Was there something else there as well?

"Colin..."

Colin stepped closer, shaking his head. "Conversation can wait, Graham."

Graham gave a shaky nod. "Let the game commence, then."

Colin blinked then nodded. Graham wrapped his arms around him, kissing his lips again. Colin's cock was stiff, hard and thick against his belly. His ass was firm and tight, and when he slipped a finger into his hole, Colin moaned softly.

Graham brought his mouth to Colin's ear. "I want to fuck you, Colin."

Colin trembled, his body warm against his. "Fuck me."

They managed to make it to the bed, crawling on their knees until they were in perfect position. Colin was in front of him, arching upright to grab on to Graham's shoulders. Graham let his hands run over his muscled chest, down his ridged belly, until he grasped Colin's cock. A bead of liquid was on the head, but it wasn't enough.

"Cream?" he rasped, nibbling on Colin's ear.

"Drawer in the bedside table," Colin whispered back.

Graham nodded. He remembered now. They'd taken one of the maids at the same time and Colin had eased into her ass with the aid of a floral-scented cream. He gave Colin's neck a nip, earning a throaty laugh from his friend, and made for the table. The little jar was inside, and Graham put a generous amount on his fingers.

He came back to Colin, holding him with one arm around his chest as he drove two fingers into his ass. Colin moaned again.

"I can't go easy tonight, I'm afraid," Graham said.

Colin nodded again. "Please, Graham."

Moving his fingers faster now, Graham felt him relax. He positioned his cock between his taut cheeks. The friction was delicious, and he couldn't wait to get inside him. He withdrew his fingers and eased the head of his cock at his hole. Closing his eyes, he pushed inside.

"Graham!" Colin pressed back, taking all of him.

Graham grunted something, he wasn't sure, then began to thrust. He prided himself on the fact that a benefit of his Hawk curse was that he could fuck forever, but tonight he was dangerously close to climax after a few strokes. Clenching his jaw tight, he held on to Colin and moved faster. It was heaven and he could feel himself beginning to lose his lauded control. He vaguely heard Colin's shouts of pleasure before he exploded inside him. They shook together, Graham trembling until he was spent.

Graham withdrew, and they collapsed on the bed as they had at the inn, but Colin was still tense. Opening one eye, he saw that he hadn't come. Well, of course he hadn't. Graham had taken everything and given nothing. That went against his rules.

"Come here," he said.

Colin turned, coming to his knees as he faced him. He sat back on his heels and brushed his black hair off his brow. His eyes still held that heat.

"What?"

Graham tilted his chin toward Colin's raging erection. Colin flushed then held himself.

"No," Graham said, coming closer. "Let me."

He took Colin's cock in his mouth, easing up and down with the care he should have taken when he'd fucked him. Cupping Colin's balls, he teased and licked before finally engulfing him in his mouth once more. Colin shouted his name again then came with a great shudder.

Colin fell back, a smile of bliss on his handsome face. "Capital," he murmured.

Graham stretched out beside him. "That was a fun romp, to be sure."

Colin stiffened and Graham cast him a glance. His brow was knit, and then he smiled. "Cracking good."

Graham was seized with the need to say something more, but for the life of him he couldn't think of a blessed thing. He'd never felt tongue-tied around Colin, so he pushed aside his unease and stretched out on his back. He pillowed his head on his hands.

"So you'll come to Hawksfell Manor with me?" he asked.

After a moment, Colin mirrored his posture. "If you truly wish it."

Graham couldn't meet his gaze, but he nodded. "I do."

"Then we shall have great fun in the Hawks' roost."

Graham released a breath he hadn't been aware he'd been holding. He knew they would rouse themselves after a few minutes. Perhaps Colin would ring for a maid to join them later. Perhaps they would just retire to the fire in the parlor downstairs. It didn't matter how they spent the rest of the evening, really.

All that mattered was that they never discuss what they'd just shared or how unsettled it made Graham feel.

Chapter 3

"Do cease vexing me, Cabot." Lily took a breath as she straightened Lady Hawksfell's chamber. "I have work to do."

"But another Hawk arrives today, Lily. Surely you're curious."

Lily shook her head and faced the footman. "And why should I be?"

Cabot winked. "I saw how you eyed the earl's brother a few months back. I bet you wanted to see if the Hawk curse was true."

Lily swallowed a retort. She had indeed wondered just that. Any of that business with the earl and his staff occurred well before she'd come here, and her mind had lots of time to wander here at the manor. She wasn't going to entertain those rumors with Cabot, though.

"You need to stop talking about the earl and his relatives, Cabot. You're going to get sacked."

Cabot stepped closer. "It's all true, you know. Even your precious Mosley has had a taste of the Hawk lusts."

Lily tamped down her reaction to the notion of the handsome chauffeur with that latest Hawk relative to come to the manor. She didn't quite know what men could do together, but she couldn't ignore the fact that the notion got her juices flowing and her blood hot.

"You're thinking about it, aren't you?" Cabot laughed. "I can see it, Lily. Your pretty white skin is flushed a lovely pink."

"Get out of the countess's room and leave me be, Cabot," she bit out.

Cabot shrugged one shoulder of his meticulously-kept livery jacket. "Fine, then. I just wanted you to prepare yourself for the earl's newest visitor."

He finally left her to her thoughts. Lily couldn't ignore the truth in some of Cabot's words. She *had* been thinking about the Hawk arriving today. There was little doubt he would be frightfully handsome. Blessed and cursed, the Hawks were. Within her earshot, Lady Hawksfell and Mr. Crowley had teased the earl about opening the manor to yet another one, but even Lily knew the earl felt an obligation. According to Cabot's well-formed and mobile mouth, ever since the earl married he'd invited many Hawks to his home. She didn't know what drove him, but it wasn't her place to wonder was it?

She left the countess's room and headed back down to the servants' hall. As she entered the common room, Mrs. Holmes stopped her.

"Guests, Lily." Mrs. Holmes smoothed her apron and patted her hair. "The earl's cousin is approaching on the drive."

Lily mimicked the housekeeper's motions and straightened her appearance by touch. She was needed out front on the drive with the other servants to welcome their newest visitor. "Yes, Mrs. Holmes."

Mrs. Holmes flashed a quick smile then shook her head. "I daresay there are more Hawks in Yorkshire than heather on the moors."

With that, the older woman left Lily to hurry up and out the front door. An impressive motor approached, the late afternoon sun glinting off the fenders. Lily found her place next to the earl's valet, Grayson. She idly noted he looked as finely turned out as Cabot and the other footman ever were. His gaze was fixed forward and his posture stiff. She mirrored his stance, grateful for the perpetuation of propriety in the sight line of both Mrs. Holmes and Mr. Carstairs, the butler. She valued this position and wouldn't let Cabot's teasing or her own foolish worries put it in jeopardy.

The sun was bright on this side of the house, thank goodness. There was little breeze, so it felt more crisp than cold on this November afternoon. She watched with deference but not much interest as the motor came to a quiet stop and the chauffeur stepped out. Yes, she was safe here at Hawksfell Manor. There was nothing or no one to change that situation. That resolve slipped as one of the prettiest men she'd ever seen stepped out onto the drive.

He had dark hair, perhaps as dark as the earl's, but that was where the comparison ended. This couldn't be the new Hawk! His features were finely wrought, and he was tall and well-built, but not nearly as large a man as all the Hawks she'd seen. His coat was of fine gray wool and spanned broad shoulders. He moved with grace as he straightened, flashing a polite smile at the assembled servants. Lily's heart gave a flutter as his blue eyes ran over her. She caught his gaze and saw that his smile didn't show in his eyes. No. In fact, he looked quite reserved. Sad, almost. She bit her lip and his brows rose. Oh, he was a risk she didn't need to take.

"Ah, the fine manor and its staff," said a deep voice.

Lily turned her attention to the large man stepping out behind the pretty one. Her heart increased its palpitations. Oh, this man in the long black coat was the Hawk most certainly. Those chiseled cheeks, that cleft chin, marked him as the earl's cousin. His hair was sun streaked instead of dark and brushed carelessly back from his forehead, but there was no mistaking the dark Hawk eyes set in his breathtakingly handsome face. Her fluttering heart dropped clear to her stomach.

She gasped, drawing his attention as well. He threw a cheeky grin in her direction, and she saw that he smiled with his entire being. He was apparently as carefree as his companion was reserved. The contrast between the two virile men caused her breath to catch. Her body tingled, and her corset suddenly felt too tight. Despite the chill, beads of sweat popped out on her chest as she flushed.

"Welcome to Hawksfell Manor, my lord," Carstairs said with a bow. "I am Carstairs, the butler."

This new Hawk mimicked his bow, and Lily saw Mrs. Holmes hide a smile behind her hand. He was a charmer to be sure, and apparently no woman was immune.

"Graham Hawk, Mr. Carstairs," he said. "Viscount Weston, actually. And this is my good friend Mr. Spencer."

The butler bowed to the viscount's friend. "The earl awaits you in his study. Will your chauffeur be staying at the manor?"

"He's my chauffeur," Mr. Spencer said. "And no, he'll return to Spencer House directly."

Lily thought about that for a moment. This Hawk's good friend lived close enough to the manor to return? She knew his motor was quite fine. She could tell that from the knowledge she'd gained during her visits to the garage when she'd been infatuated with the earl's last chauffeur. Mr. Spencer was obviously as well-heeled as any Hawk. Two extraordinarily attractive, wealthy men were to stay at the manor for an indeterminate amount of time. Men who were undoubtedly used to getting what they wanted when they wanted it. Her traitorous body heated. Their eyes ran over her body again and her drawers grew damp. *God save me.*

"Will your men be joining you?" Carstairs asked.

The earl shook his head. "I'm afraid my valet is at Weston Park."

"Mine is at Spencer House," Mr. Spencer said.

Mr. Carstairs nodded. "If it will serve, Cabot can look after you both during your stay."

He indicated the cocky footman, who straightened with a deferential expression on his face. The two visitors nodded their agreement, and Cabot threw a wink in her direction. Lily kept her face impassive even as the image of both lovely men in various stages of undress danced through her fevered mind.

They walked past her as Carstairs led them into the manor, and she caught a bit of their divergent scents. Mr. Spencer's was fresh and hot, like mint tea. The viscount's was more deeper, like the touch of spice with a touch of sweet. Both combined to set her head spinning. She must have swayed, for Grayson caught her elbow.

"Are you all right, Lily?" he asked in a low voice.

Her cheeks flaming, she nodded. "I slipped a bit on the gravel," she said in answer.

Grayson nodded and released her, looking forward once again. Lily absently noticed that the rest of the servants filed back into the house behind Carstairs and Mrs. Holmes, and forced her own feet to move. She thanked the Lord she didn't have to serve at table.

However could she bear to be close to two such men?

* * * *

Graham eyed the pretty maid as he walked past the line of Hawksfell servants. Her eyes were such an unusual shade of green, and when she'd bitten that full lower lip, he'd felt a flash of heat. Not since last night with Colin had he experienced such a swift rush of lust. He lowered his gaze and followed the butler into the manor.

Hawksfell was impressive, of tall sandstone walls and topped with a many-peaked slate roof. The earl was gifted with money, no doubt. Colin had said so, knowledge he'd gleaned from the gossip he'd heard over the years, but the evidence before him still surprised. Was the earl still plagued with their curse as well as their blessing?

As they walked further into the manor, Graham noticed that the maids who had stood so still on the drive now peeked around the corners at him and Colin. He didn't see the green-eyed girl, though. He idly wondered how many of the maids, and the male servants for that matter, the earl had fucked over the years. Had he taken the very pretty green-eyed one?

"The earl awaits you in his study, my lord," the butler said. "Mr. Spencer, I'll have one of the footman show you to your room. The earl said to place you both in the bachelor wing."

Colin met Graham's gaze then nodded. Cabot, the man given to both of them for the length of their visit, indicated the wide staircase and Colin ascended. Graham felt relieved, and a bit guilty. The ride from Spencer House had been strained, even though he had done his level best to keep the mood light. Last night had been incredible, but he wouldn't talk about it. Thankfully, Colin didn't seem bent on exploring the topic, either.

"Viscount Weston, my lord," Carstairs said, breaking through to Graham.

The butler stepped back, and Graham stepped into the Earl of Hawksfell's study. It was a handsome room, masculine and as well-appointed as the bit of the manor he'd seen thus far. A large desk dominated the space, as did the tall man who stood when he entered.

"Viscount Weston," the earl said with a slight smile.

Graham blinked. Aside from the hair, it was like looking in a mirror. "Lord Hawksfell."

Carstairs closed the door as he left, and the earl waved toward the armchair facing the desk. "Sit, please. And call me Gabriel."

Graham smiled. "Gabriel. Then you must call me Graham."

Gabriel sat, and Graham did likewise.

"So another Hawk cousin has accepted my invitation."

"I'll admit I was curious to meet you, Gabriel. My friend Mr. Spencer told me of some interesting developments up here at the manor over the past few months." He winked. "And something about the previous few years?"

Gabriel's cheeks flushed, and then he shook his head. "I take it Mr. Spencer lives in the local environs?"

He smiled. "Not far, yes."

"And the two of you are close?"

Graham managed to nod.

Gabriel narrowed his eyes, and for a moment Graham felt like he could see through his smile to his own uncertainty about this whole visit. Had he been wrong to come here?

Gabriel smiled himself and gave a sharp nod, leaning back in his chair. "I've had your things put in a room in the bachelor wing, yours and Mr. Spencer's as well. I'd like to clarify the misconceptions about my life here at the manor, Graham."

Graham held up a hand. "You owe me no explanations, Gabriel. You are the head of this family, really. I feel honored that you wished to extend this invitation. I look forward to getting to know you and your family."

Gabriel's smile was warmer now. "My family, yes. I'll admit the curse ruled me before I fell in love."

"I daresay I cannot wait to meet your countess."

"My brother lives on the property as well, and you now have cousins situated not so far away. More Hawks, as it were."

"So Colin told me." It was passing strange that so many Hawks seemed to have found some sort of life for themselves in the shadow of the manor, but Graham wasn't going to pretend that such a life was meant for him. "It's commendable, I suppose."

"Commendable?" Gabriel frowned. "Marriage is far more than commendable, Graham. It can be most preferable to what life was like before."

"And I'm quite certain it suits you and your brother." Graham felt flustered, feeling his façade slipping a bit. "And our Hawk cousins, I suppose."

"Then you've never been tempted to get leg-shackled?"

Graham laughed, forcing a bit more frivolity into the sound than he felt. "Hardly! You're a Hawk, Gabriel. We fuck. It's what we do. It's what we have to do."

"I'm not denying that." Gabriel's expression smoothed. "My staff is at your disposal. Yours and Mr. Spencer's."

Graham's mouth dropped open. "Then it's all true? You fuck your staff?"

"I *fucked* my staff. Often and out of necessity. That's changed for me."

"And yet, they are still..." He couldn't bring himself to say what he was thinking. They were chattel meant to ease the earl and nothing more?

"They are my staff, Graham. Loyal and discreet. I no longer

require their sensual service, as it were. That doesn't mean that if they are of like mind you cannot avail yourself to one…or more of them."

Again, the image of the little green-eyed maid popped into his mind. Her skin had flushed when he'd passed close to her. He'd seen the smooth skin of her cheek, her throat, turn pink and watched her full lips part. Would she let him fuck her? Would she let Colin?

"I thank you then, Gabriel." He cleared his throat. "For your hospitality, of course."

"You are very welcome." Gabriel came to his feet. "Perhaps you can find a way to break your own curse. It's been known to happen."

Graham stood and shook the earl's hand. "I have no such illusions."

Gabriel looked as though he was going to say something more, to wax poetic of marriage and how delightful it was to have one person forever. Then he gave another nod Graham was already coming to know was a customary gesture of his.

"We'll see you at dinner, then." Gabriel arched a brow. "You and your good friend?"

"We shall have a fine time, I wager." Graham sketched a bow and grinned. "At dinner and, perhaps, after."

Gabriel seemed to take his jest at face value and laughed softly. "Quite."

Graham left the earl's study and one of the ever-present servants showed him to his room. It was finely appointed, with a very large bed and an adjacent dressing room and bath. He saw that his things had been arranged, and he was all but settled for a long visit. He sat on the edge of the bed and thought about his strange conversation with the earl.

Gabriel had given him permission to take any and all of his staff, as long as they were willing. It was strange to think of all the cocks and pussies at his disposal. He brushed his hair back from his face and blew out a breath. What was he to do with the opportunity presented? Surely Colin would be up for a romp. The passion they'd shared was astounding, even though it left him feeling strangely vulnerable afterward. They could see just how many of the earl's dedicated and circumspect staff they could fuck before their visit ended.

"We'll make a game of it," he told himself.

Then perhaps he could get back on more stable ground with Colin. Both in bed and out of it.

Chapter 4

Colin joined Graham in his guest room after dining with the earl and his family. The room was as fine as his own, done in burgundy and gold where his was done in blue and silver. A cheery fire burned behind the grate, and he knew he would find his room as comfortable when he retired.

"Dinner was…interesting," Colin said, loosening his tie.

Graham appeared perplexed, his brow furrowed in an expression Colin had rarely seen before their visit to Hawksfell Manor. He sat down in one of the armchairs that flanked the fireplace and stretched out his long legs. "Imagine, all that bloody happiness."

Colin had seen the true love evidently shared by the earl and his wife, but couldn't ignore the link between the couple and her third cousin. More "bloody happiness," he supposed.

"What do you make of Mr. Crowley?" Colin asked, sitting across from him. He was introduced as the countess's third cousin, but it was clear there was affection between him and the beautiful lady of the manor as well as obvious attraction to the earl.

Graham shrugged. "I'm not sure what you're asking."

Colin snorted. "Aren't you?"

Graham blinked. "You don't suppose the three of them…?"

"I most certainly do. It's obvious the countess loves both of them."

"But does she fuck both of them?" Graham held up a hand. "No, no. I shouldn't be thinking of my host and his family that way."

"She is gorgeous," Colin observed. "So is her cousin, not to mention the earl. And she appears very happy."

"Happy." Again Graham wore that look of consternation.

"I can scarcely wait to meet the rest of your Hawk relatives."

Graham's brows shot up. "Do you suppose they also...? Well, Hawks have always fucked anything and everything. Why shouldn't that extend to the marriage bed?"

Colin wanted to ask if he would ever consider such a thing in the future. Perhaps if Graham could find a woman to make his viscountess, his own Hawk beast would be satisfied. The prospect left him feeling unsettled, though.

"So what are we about on this visit?" he asked, eager to change the subject of Hawks and their implausible marriages. "You were closed up with the earl for some time this afternoon."

"He confirmed what you told me, Colin." Graham's dark eyes sparkled, and he leaned forward. "The manor is staffed with the willing and able."

Colin felt a flicker of desire course through him. "The maids, Graham?"

"Maids?" Graham chuckled. "You saw her, then. One particular maid in that row of starch and submission?"

"The green-eyed girl. Hell yes, I saw her."

"She would be a good one to start with, I think. From her position in the line, I would wager she's the countess's maid."

"A lady's maid." Colin thought for moment. "Higher than we usually take."

Graham laughed out loud. "When has any woman been able to refuse either of us?"

"Too true."

"You remember that baron's sister? Well, she fell easily enough." Graham rubbed his hands together. "Let's make a game of it. See how many of the earl's staff will succumb to our combined charms."

"Seems a bit mercenary, no?"

"Not at all. We'll leave them happy. Have we ever left anyone wanting for pleasure?"

He thought about the maid they'd shared at the inn and saw the truth of Graham's words. "But the thought of a game..."

Graham's brows drew together. "No one will get hurt, Colin."

Colin forced a smile. *No one will get hurt?* He thought back to their night together, a night Graham had apparently put behind him. "Very well, then." He stood. "I'll bid you good night."

"Good night." Graham closed his eyes and let his head fall back. "Yes, they keep country hours here it seems."

Colin left Graham to his thoughts and returned to his own guest room. There was something here at the manor. Was it the obvious love among their host, his wife and her cousin? Perhaps. There was a tempting sort of happiness here. It drew him, and he wasn't even a Hawk. What would it do to Graham?

Things were about to change. Graham's Hawk legacy couldn't be ignored. But where, then, did that leave him?

* * * *

In the morning Graham was once more struck by the open affection in the breakfast room. As he'd noted last evening to Colin, the earl and his family rose early. Afterward Gabriel asked Graham to accompany him into the village. Considering it a lark, he agreed. He hadn't expected the earl's brother and the countess's cousin to come along, though. Colin declined the invitation. Though he felt a niggle of guilt, he was a bit relieved he wouldn't be faced with the intimacy he and his friend had shared that last night at his house.

Colin had seemed preoccupied last night, and Graham suspected he'd wanted to ask just what the hell that had been between them. Aside from more mind-shattering pleasure than he could have imagined, he had no idea. He certainly didn't want to discuss it. Not when he still felt unsettled about it himself.

The trip proved pleasant, and to his surprise he found that the earl's brother was a bit more easygoing than Gabriel. In fact, Matthew

Hawk spoke of a masked ball held at the manor where he played a game that Graham surely would have enjoyed. Inviting his lovers to attend in disguise? That would be something indeed.

Perhaps he could play that particular game with Colin and the little green-eyed maid. He didn't need a ball to set the scene, though. No, his fine guest room would be most fitting for all sorts of games. The prospect made his cock twitch in anticipation. Ah, his Hawk beast would be soothed by this visit to the manor.

When they returned to the house, Graham hung back at the garage. All this unusual familiarity was grating after a while. God knew he never had any real warmth with his great aunt and uncle, and aside from Colin he had no one constant friend in his life. The closeness caused a funny feeling in his belly, and he thought a walk in the brisk autumn air might help clear his head. Besides, he definitely couldn't face his friend right now.

The day was chilly, and much grayer than yesterday. As he strolled he wondered how Colin was getting on in the great house alone. Maybe he was reading in the library or seeing to correspondence. The man was as successful as he himself was, title or no. Surely he had to see to business despite this visit.

As Graham rounded the side of the garage, a woman's cry reached him. He hurried toward the voice, alarm zipping along his nerves. After rounding the corner to the secluded back of the building, he halted. He saw it was the pretty green-eyed maid and she was being cozied up to against the back wall of the carriage house by the valet he and Colin shared. From his vantage point ten feet away he could see that the valet wasn't doing much more than teasing the girl. Cabot's hands were a bit too friendly on her curves—hell, she had very nice curves—but he wasn't going to step in and bring a halt to the couple's fun. He swiftly turned to go.

"Stop it!" she cried, her voice reedy and thin.

He turned again to find Cabot pulling on her apron strings as she twisted away from him. The valet appeared to be jesting, but the maid's face showed her fear. Whatever game Cabot was about, it was obvious she didn't want to play along. Her cheeks were chalk white, and her incredible eyes were opened wide as she trembled. Not wanting to frighten her further, he forced himself to walk instead of run toward them.

"Out for a bit of sport, Cabot?" he drawled.

The valet dropped her apron strings like they burned him. "Lord Weston," he said, bowing his head.

The maid slumped against the wall now, her breath coming fast as she fumbled with the apron. Graham quickly ran his eyes over her but didn't see anything else amiss, other than a few strands of her mahogany hair loose from the bun at the back of her head.

He faced the valet. "Perhaps there is someplace you need to be, Cabot?"

Without another glance at the maid, the valet bowed again and hurried away from the garage toward the back of the house. Graham turned back to the maid. She was shaking, tears glistening on her cheeks. His stomach twisted.

"He's gone," he told her. "There's nothing to fear."

"He was just playing," she murmured, her voice flat.

"What's that?" Graham asked.

She raised her eyes to meet his. "Cabot." She swallowed. "I know he was just teasing, but I…" Her eyes widened as she focused on him. "Oh! Forgive me, my lord."

Straightening, she turned to go. He caught her apron strings as she tried to run past him and she gasped.

"Your apron," he said in explanation. As he tied the strings around her slender waist, he could feel the rigidity in her body. "I'm not playing like Cabot, love."

She whirled and looked up at him. "What?"

He held out his hands palms up. "I was just tying your apron."

She gave a shaky nod, running her hands over her wrinkled apron.

He took her trembling hands in his. "Your hands are like ice.

Were you truly that frightened of that boy?"

"No, no." She breathed in, her gaze sliding from his. "I knew he was teasing. It just reminded me of…"

"Reminded you of what?" Graham had to ask.

She raised a hand to tuck a thick strand of hair behind one delicate ear. "Excuse me, my lord."

"You cannot mean to return to the house in this condition."

Her hands were suddenly frantic, running over her hair and uniform as her cheeks paled again. Once again, he took her hands in his. "Easy…" He smiled down at her. "What's your name?"

"Lily."

He blinked. How fitting. She was delicate and exotic and so bloody beautiful. He stroked her cheek. "Your skin is as soft as a flower petal, Lily."

She bit her bottom lip, her teeth very white against her plump, rosy flesh. "My lord…"

"Graham," he corrected, bringing his face to hers. "I'm not 'my lord' out here, love."

"Out here." She swallowed, and he watched the motion move the muscles of her throat. "I shouldn't be out here."

Graham shook his head. "You serve only the countess. She can't need you right now."

"How do you know that?" Her voice was low, breathy.

"You're a lady's maid." He moved his lips over her smooth cheek to her ear. "It's hours until the time to dress for dinner."

She closed her eyes and leaned her head away from him, exposing herself to his lips. He didn't miss the invitation, and dragged his tongue along the smooth tendon at the base of her neck.

"Mmm, you smell like lilies," he rasped.

"Oh," she sighed.

His Hawk beast rose as his cock filled in an instant. He lifted his head and glanced about, swiftly noting that no one was about or could see them from the house. He couldn't take her out here, though. He was all for fun and games, but he wouldn't fuck her outside. For one thing, it might not be cold this afternoon but it wasn't exactly temperate.

"Come with me, sweet Lily," he said, grabbing her hand and tugging her toward him. "I have to taste you, and I will not let the chill of the breeze touch what I guess must be skin even softer than your neck."

Chapter 5

Lily shouldn't go with this man. She knew that. Yet she permitted Lord Weston to tug her along behind him as he entered the back of the garage. As they stepped into the darkened interior, he skidded to a stop, looking about with his broad shoulders tense. He visibly relaxed after a moment.

"Ah, good." He turned and smiled down at her. "I suspected the chauffeur would be up at the house after bringing us back from the village."

She just stared up into the intensity burning in his dark Hawk eyes. He was the most handsome one she'd ever met. Even the earl's brother couldn't touch him in sheer magnetism. That must be why she was here with him now. That, and the way he'd made her feel safe after Cabot's fumbled attempt at seduction.

The viscount had been gentle and strong at the same time. Cabot hadn't been attacking her. She knew that in her mind. But the situation had felt far too much like that last night under the old baron's roof. Her heart had raced and her body felt cold.

Yes, the viscount made her feel safe out there in the yard. However, she was honest enough with herself to admit that wasn't why she was standing here with him now. It was his sensual pull that drew her.

"Thank you, my lord," she said, lifting her chin with what she prayed was a gesture of strength.

"You're welcome, of course." He removed his coat and took her hands again. "And call me Graham."

"I couldn't."

"You most certainly can." He drew her close, his spicy, hot scent wrapping around her despite the oily scent of metal that hung in the clean garage. "When I make you come, I want to hear you say my name."

His words were shocking, yet they sent a stab of want through her body. Her drawers grew damp and her nipples tightened in her corset. "My lord…"

He brought his lips to her neck again, stroking with that very clever tongue of his. "Graham, Lily." He nipped her earlobe. "Call me 'Graham.'"

His hands were on her waist, loosening her apron again and working the buttons of her uniform blouse free. When his fingers brushed the tops of her breasts she gasped. "Graham."

She could feel him smile against her skin. As he danced her back up against the nearest wall, she was soon grateful for its support.

He brought his mouth to hers and flicked his tongue over her lips. "Mmm, soft."

She parted her lips, and his tongue surged inside. She froze, remembering the horrid kisses the old baron had forced on her. Then she tasted only Lord Weston. The latest Hawk. Graham. She leaned into him and touched her tongue to his. When he groaned, she felt a surge of power she'd never felt that terrible long-ago night.

Graham loosened her corset, and she felt a rush of cool air on her breasts. Then one large hand of his cupped her, squeezing gently. His mouth left hers, and he glanced down at her breasts. Her nipples hardened almost painfully.

"You're a pretty package, Lily," he said, rubbing his thumb over the nipple he held captive. "I have to taste you."

His mouth closed over her nipple, and she let her eyes drift closed. Hot, wet suction pulled at her. Her body trembled, and she clutched at his shoulders. He fondled her other breast with sure fingers, and the pressure was exquisite. Her body began to pulse. Her fingers ran through his gold-streaked hair, and she arched toward him.

"Oh, my!"

He smiled again. She was sure of it.

He lifted his head from her aching flesh to bring his brow to hers. "Do you like what I'm doing, Lily love?"

She could only nod. He kissed her lips and moved closer still. Her skirt rustled as he drew it up over her legs, and she didn't protest when his fingers caressed her through her drawers.

"Your pussy's wet," he rasped. "Delightful."

He brought his mouth to her breast again as he removed her drawers.

Her thighs parted, and she welcomed his touch. "Make me…come, Graham."

He murmured something in response and two fingers thrust inside her. It was amazing, this pleasure he was intent on giving her. His thumb brushed over her clit, and she bit back a scream. Every nerve was singing as her body drew tighter and tighter.

"Graham!"

She came in the next moment, clutching at his shoulders as she bucked hard against his hand. She'd never known pleasure before, or guessed it could be like this. It was hot and sharp, and her body craved more of it.

"Christ," he said, coming up to kiss her. "I have to have you."

She couldn't resist as he unbuttoned his trousers. His cock surged free, huge and hard and hot against her bare thighs. He seemed to hesitate, so she arched toward him.

"Please," she whispered.

Without another word, he parted her legs further and drove deep inside her. His thrusts were forceful, his passion high as he pounded into her. "Lily, Lily, Lily."

She took all of him high up inside her as she moved with him. Soon she was cresting swiftly toward the second orgasm of her life. Moaning his name, she climaxed around his hard shaft.

He shuddered against her then poured himself inside. His breath was harsh against her ear, his arms still braced on the wall behind her. His weight was a comfort, though. It grounded her after the madness of her incredible release.

"That was amazing," he said, kissing her neck. "I knew you were wet and suspected you would be hot. But you're so damn tight."

She felt her cheeks flame, which was odd since the two of them were still so intimately connected. "I…"

"You held my cock like a fist, love." He withdrew, tucking himself back inside his trousers. "You made me forget myself. I haven't come inside a woman in I don't even know how long."

She absently nodded as she did some mental calculations. She wasn't near the vulnerable time of her cycle. Surely this aberration wouldn't have consequences.

When she finally opened her eyes again, he was staring down at her.

"Are you all right?" He cupped her face gently. "I can sometimes go a bit mad." He winked. "I am a Hawk, after all."

He had been mad, his lust so great he'd wrung sharp passion out of her with his power. It was a blissful madness. It seemed forward to admit that, though.

"I'm fine," she said in a small voice.

"Good." He grinned and her heart flipped. "I daresay we're going to do that again."

Her mouth dropped open. "Pardon?"

"I don't know how long I'm here at Hawksfell, Lily." He kissed her hard as if he couldn't help himself, then pulled back. "I know I'm going to want to play more games with you."

She couldn't say anything to that. This was a game? Well, she wasn't foolish enough to believe their coupling meant anything more. Perhaps calling it a game would suffice. It would certainly make a pleasant memory for her once he'd left Hawksfell Manor.

"We'll just see about that," she managed to say, once more evoking an expression of worldliness.

He blinked then laughed at her challenge. "Splendid." He helped her straighten her uniform and tied her apron. "There. Right as rain. Now go."

There was a twinkle of something else in his eyes, but she couldn't think about that right now. She had to get back up to the house and change for the evening before seeing to the countess. She nodded and hurried out of the garage.

It was only when she gained her attic room that she realized she wasn't wearing her drawers.

* * * *

Colin returned to his room to ready for dinner. He'd spent the day in various mundane occupations, such as penning a few letters and seeing to the estate papers that always seemed to dog his steps. The earl's staff was most accommodating, though the place felt rather like a tomb when no one was about.

He'd wondered how Graham fared in the village with the other Hawks. Surely he'd charmed them with his quick wit and joviality. Graham was a pleasant companion in any situation. It was one of his defining characteristics, that spark and charisma of his. It was what had first drawn a shy Colin to him at school and what kept them friends these many years. Well, that and the insatiable appetite for flesh they both shared.

An unusually dour Cabot came in and assisted Colin. His movements were stiff and his eyes downcast.

"Cabot, is something troubling you?" he asked.

"Nothing, Mr. Spencer." Cabot finished with Colin's shirt and tie and eased his jacket over his shoulders. "Will there be anything else?"

"I take it you've already seen to Lord Weston?"

For some reason Colin couldn't fathom, the valet paled. "Yes, Mr. Spencer. I'm wanted downstairs to help with dinner service."

"Go, then." Colin smiled. "I wouldn't want to make you late."

Cabot bowed and hurried out of the room. "Good evening, Lord Weston."

"Good evening," Graham said in response. He walked into Colin's guest room and closed the door. "Hello, Colin."

Colin straightened the tie Cabot had tied a little hastily. "What the devil did you do to Cabot?"

Graham waved a hand. "Put a bit of fear into him, is all."

Colin brushed his hair back and turned from the mirror. "Whatever for?"

Graham chuckled. "For trying to snatch a choice biscuit not meant for him."

"You'll have to elaborate, Graham. What biscuit, precisely?"

Graham's eyes sparkled, and Colin knew.

"The little green-eyed maid?" he asked.

Graham nodded. "And she smells as sweet as her name, Colin."

Colin smiled. "Which is?"

"Lily." Graham's lids lowered as he obviously relished the memory. "Sweet, exotic Lily."

"Never say you fucked her."

Graham shrugged. "I hadn't meant to. But after she came around my fingers I couldn't resist."

Colin imagined Graham and the gorgeous maid and felt a lick of lust along his groin. "Where?"

"In the garage. Not ideal, but it was opportune." He reached into his pocket and withdrew a bit of linen trimmed with lace. "Kept her drawers."

Colin laughed. "As a memento?"

"As a promise." He brought her drawers to his nose and sniffed. "She's so sweet. I told her I'd have her again and, to my surprise and delight, she issued me a challenge. She seems up for the game."

Graham tossed him her drawers, and Colin caught them. They still felt a bit damp. "Our game?" Again, Colin felt flush with desire as the scent of the girl's passion reached him.

"Of course. She seems to think she can resist, silly girl."

"Graham, was she all right after?"

"Of course." Graham's brow knit. "Although…"

"What?"

"When I came upon Cabot trying to have a taste, she looked almost terrified."

"What was he doing to her?"

"Nothing, really. Just teasing."

"Maybe she was a virgin."

Graham slanted him a look. "She wasn't. Besides, I wouldn't have fucked her against the wall if that were the case."

Colin thought about their conversation of just how they would spend this visit to Hawksfell Manor. "So it's her, then?"

Graham nodded.

"What about your notion of bagging as many servants as possible?"

Graham shook his head. "She'll prove more than enough, I wager. We'll just have to see if she'll play along with us."

Colin's stomach clenched. "Us?"

Graham's eyes were intent. "I don't want to take her alone again, Colin." Then he winked, the jester back in play. "In fact, I can't wait to watch you fuck her."

Colin smiled, as eager for the game now as Graham was, and tossed her drawers back to him. "*Will* she play along, do you think?"

"She runs hot. The hottest we've had in a long time. It didn't take much to set her to boiling."

Colin thought for a moment. "She's the countess's maid."

"Yes. What matter is that? I thought we discussed that already."

"I know, I know. She has no reason to be about the bachelors' wing, though."

Graham stuck his hands in his pockets and began to pace. "Her duties with the countess don't draw much on her time. From what little I know about Gabriel's wife, she is no prima donna who must be attended to constantly. Finding Lily out by the garage in the afternoon might attest to that."

An idea struck Colin. "We can say we have mending and without our valets here we prefer a maid's hand to a footman's."

Graham grinned. "That is most imperious of you, Mr. Spencer."

Colin shrugged. "Should that trait be reserved for Hawks only?"

Graham laughed. "Not at all, friend."

"Then let's go to dinner. It's a shame, but I believe I might just tear my cuff this evening."

Graham chuckled as they went down to the parlor to await the dinner bell.

Chapter 6

Lily sat in the servants' hall the next afternoon, trying to still her pulse while the events of the past day ran circles through her mind. She hadn't needed to serve at the table last night, thank the Lord. No, the others always saw to the family upstairs in the dining room. There had been more Hawks here last night as well. The earl's brother and one of his cousins had joined the party, along with their wives. She knew that Posy, the former parlor maid, had been up there, too. The wife to the earl's brother. How did that girl feel, no longer serving the Hawks but now one of them? If Lily hadn't seen the obvious love between her and Matthew Hawk when he'd first arrived as the earl's guest two months ago, she never would have believed the truth of it.

In a flash, Graham Hawk came into her mind. Oh, what she'd let him do. What she'd begged him to do! It wasn't like her. She wasn't a girl to throw her favors around. The fact that she hadn't been here before the earl's marriage was immaterial in her opinion. She wouldn't have given herself to Lord Hawksfell in any event. Of course, were that particular condition part of her employment at the time she'd been hired she might not be working in the manor right now. Sex was the very last thing she'd wanted to consider after leaving her last position.

"Lily, Mr. Spencer needs you," Mrs. Holmes said from the doorway.

"Pardon?" She blinked as an impression of Graham's lovely friend popped into her mind right alongside his image. "Whatever for?"

Mrs. Holmes folded her hands over her midsection. "It seems he has some mending to be seen to."

"Can't Cabot see to him? I thought he was taking care of him and the viscount during their stay."

The housekeeper's brow knit. "Cabot is not a valet, Lily. He's serving in a pinch, as it were."

Lily knew the woman was right. Cabot was ham-handed at best and wouldn't be able to handle fine work.

"What about Grayson?" Lily asked, hoping the earl's valet could see to one of his guests in this regard.

"Grayson is the earl's man, Lily," Mrs. Holmes answered.

Lily swallowed her disappointment. The earl's valet would never look after his guests' mending. She was well and truly stuck, then.

"I'll go retrieve his mending," she said with restrained resignation.

Mrs. Holmes nodded and turned, obviously already set on her next task. "He's staying in the blue room."

"Yes, Mrs. Holmes."

Lily stood and smoothed her hands over her apron. She glanced in the small glass set on one wall and saw that her hair was neat and her cap straight. Her uniform was crisp and she wore her drawers today. A wave of heat rushed over her as she remembered the moment when she'd realized the viscount had kept them. For what purpose? As part of his "game," perhaps? Though it was strange to admit, the notion of him keeping something so intimate of hers made her body tingle.

She made her way up two flights of stairs until she was in the bachelor wing of the manor. The blue room was on the left side of the hallway and as she raised her hand to knock she caught a bit of Graham's spiciness in the air. He was surely staying across the hall. Holding her breath, she knocked softly but got no answer. Breathing once again, she pushed open the door and was struck by Mr. Spencer's hint of fresh scent. It was heavier here than Graham's had been in the hall, yet the two scents seemed to mingle in her head to take her breath once more.

A few pieces of clothing were resting on the chair near the low dressing table. She crossed to the table and picked up a shirt that was missing a button and a jacket that had a small tear on the cuff. The jacket was as finely made as what the viscount had worn yesterday. She remembered grabbing on to his jacket and holding him close as he'd taken her, the material caressing her fingers as he buried himself deep inside of her.

She closed her eyes and brought the jacket to her nose and sniffed. Oh, Mr. Spencer's smell was as intoxicating as Graham's. Swaying slightly, she felt her pussy pulse as it had in the garage. Oh, what if Mr. Spencer touched her? Her nipples tightened, and she let out a sigh.

"It seems Lord Weston was correct," a masculine voice said.

She opened her eyes and clutched the clothing in her hands. The pretty dark-haired man was standing very close. How had he come so near without her knowledge? "Mr. Spencer!"

He tilted his head and smiled. It was a lovely smile, really. "You called Graham by his given name, Lily. Can't you afford me the same boon?"

She bit her lip as she recalled just when she'd done that. Oh, his mouth had been on her breasts! Nibbling and licking and driving her mad. "Mr. Spencer, I—"

"Colin, love," he corrected.

She turned, her bottom pressed against the table as she brought the pile of mending close to her chest. "I shouldn't be in here. Not when you're present."

He reached up to stroke her cheek. "But I asked for you."

She resisted the urge to lean into his hand. His touch was soft yet insistent. "To fetch your mending."

"And what of my trousers? Will you see to them?"

She glanced down to see an obvious bulge in the fabric at his crotch and squeezed her eyes shut. "Mr. Spencer..."

"Colin." His hands moved to her neck, his fingers nimble on her skin. "You're making my cock hard, Lily. Careful, or you'll be mending the seams of my pants."

Her mouth dropped open, and he brought his lips to hers. Oh, his taste! His tongue surged inside and she caught his moan. Here was the passion she'd had with Graham. How could she feel it for this man, too?

She didn't care. "Oh, Colin!"

Dropping his clothes to the floor, she gripped his broad shoulders. He held her closer now, his hands on her bottom as he pressed his cock firmly against the juncture of her thighs. Burying his face in her neck, he licked the skin just above her collar.

"You are sweet," he rasped. "Graham was right."

She froze, her eyes snapping open. "Graham?"

He lifted his head. Gently grasping her chin, he looked deep into her eyes. "He told me about the game, Lily."

"G–game?"

He nodded. "You issued a challenge, love. That you could resist."

She shook her head. "I never—"

"Then you admit defeat?"

She stared into his bright blue eyes, her legs going weak. "I don't know how to play this game," she admitted on a whisper.

"Never fear," Graham said, stepping out of Colin's dressing room. "We'll be happy to teach you."

He looked as good as Colin did, strong and broad and even larger here in the blue room. Graham stepped behind her and untied her apron. Colin began to work the buttons of her blouse free, tugging it from the waistband of her skirt as Graham drew her skirt up over her legs. His hands brushed the sensitive skin of her inner thighs, bringing to mind all he'd done to her in the garage. She shivered as she felt her pussy swell.

"Oh…" she sighed.

"I can smell you," Graham said. "Colin, can you smell her?"

Colin brought his nose to the swell of her breasts. "Mmm, yes."

Her nipples tightened as he dragged his tongue just beneath the edge of her corset. Gripping the dressing table at her back, she leaned her head back and prayed he'd take what she offered. To her delight and relief, he did. He loosened her corset and cupped her breast, tugging on her nipple. Sharp pleasure spiked through her.

"I want to taste you, Lily," Graham said, dropping to his knees in front of her. He tore her drawers from her and flicked his tongue over her clit. "You're even sweeter here."

He stroked her flesh as Colin fondled her nipple. While his mouth tugged and nibbled on her breast, Graham became more forceful on her pussy. His tongue drove into her as his thumb worked her clit. Colin's mouth pulled at one nipple as he pinched the other. She couldn't hold on to a thought as they both used their mouths and fingers to set her on fire. She couldn't catch her breath as Graham lifted her up on her toes.

"Come for us, Lily," Colin said, moving on to the other breast. "Come."

She bit her lip to hold back a scream as her orgasm shot through her. Graham's hands were firm on her bottom as he drew out every pulse and shudder. Colin finally released her breast and brought his mouth to hers again.

"That was lovely," he said, smiling down at her.

Graham gave her clit one last long lick that made her shiver. Her legs were weak and her body flushed. At this moment she didn't care about her position at the manor. She didn't care about her future with either of these gentlemen. No. At the moment, with her heartbeat still erratic and her body replete, she only cared about the game.

* * * *

Graham stood, growling as he cupped himself. His cock was pounding, his beast wild after tasting Lily. "Sweet Lily," he said, coming up to kiss her. He wanted to fuck her right now, but one look at Colin and he knew he had to let him have the next ride. He needed relief, though. He teased her full lower lip and grinned. "Suck me, Lily."

She blinked those amazing green eyes, her lush lips parted. "S–suck...?"

He shared a look with Colin, who nodded. "Colin will take you tonight, love."

Their girl stared at him and gave a small nod, almost as if she wasn't aware of the gesture. Colin's expression sharpened, and Graham knew his friend wanted her pussy wrapped around his cock. He couldn't blame him. He'd never felt a cunt so tight in his life.

"Show her what you need, Graham," Colin said, his voice low.

She looked from one to the other then settled her gaze on his trousers. He couldn't wait another moment as he tore at the buttons on his trousers. His cock was free in his hand now, hot and hard and eager for her pretty mouth. He had to lean against the dressing table himself, every bit of his strength seeming to flow into his shaft. "Suck me, Lily," he said again. "Please?"

Blinking, she seemed to envision it. Her tongue peeped out to lick her lips, and he almost came. With a whimper, a sound of surrender or need, she fell to her knees and closed her mouth around him.

It was heaven, her lips tight on his shaft as her tongue danced over the head. He dug his fingers into her thick, shining hair, scattering pins and letting her little lace cap fall to the floor. She was moaning now, the act apparently causing her body to heat.

"Fuck her, Colin," he managed to say on a groan.

Colin lifted Lily off her knees, but she never broke contact on Graham's cock. Colin maneuvered her in front of him and flipped up her skirt. He fingered her, and she moaned around Graham's cock. It was a delicious sound and an incredible sensation.

"Ah, Lily. I want to feel your pussy, love," Colin said. "Graham said you're so tight."

She arched toward Colin, nodding and sending a new pulse of pleasure down to Graham's balls. Graham watched as Colin freed himself. Colin's eyes were intent, and Graham could well imagine the view. Her lips would be swollen from the orgasm he'd given her, but now they'd open for Colin's cock. He held his breath, eager for the sight of Colin pounding into her tender flesh.

Colin held onto her slender hips and sank into her. He threw his head back as he moved, faster and faster until all three of them were panting.

"I'm coming!" Graham shouted, coming into her mouth in hot spurts.

She licked him one more time then lifted her head. "Oh, my!" Her legs shook as she gripped the table, one hand on each side of Graham's hips.

Colin was balls-deep, his head thrown back as his body worked her. She was close. Graham knew it. He drew her slightly up to him, kissing her swollen mouth as Colin continued to fuck her. Reaching down between her legs, he pinched her clit. She screamed as she came, bucking wildly as Colin joined her in climax.

He kissed her again, stroking her hair back from her sweat-damp brow. "Did you like the game tonight?"

She nodded to him then straightened to throw her arms around Colin. "That was lovely!"

Colin grinned, his cheeks ruddy. "At the risk of echoing Graham, we're going to do that again."

She seemed to swoon, but neither he nor Colin missed it when she whispered the word *yes.* He might not know what was going on between him and his best friend after their night together, but he knew this girl could please them both.

Maybe, just maybe, she could help them figure out where this game was leading.

Chapter 7

"What are Graham's plans, Gabriel?"

The countess's innocent question made Lily start. She fumbled a bit, but neither Lady Hawksfell nor the earl seemed to notice anything amiss in her demeanor. She kept her back to them just in case, though. Her cheeks were warm, but she supposed that could be attributed to her close proximity to the fire. The morning's chill could be felt if you stood close to the windows today, so no one would think it odd that she sought out the warmth of the hearth.

"My cousin isn't about to confide in me, Millicent," the earl answered.

Lily watched him out of the corner of her eye, seeing the stark similarities between him and Graham. Same striking features, dark eyes, and cleft chin. His hair was a lustrous black like Colin's, though. Oh, her silly head was muddled from the incredible pleasure the two friends had given her in the blue room. Imagine, two men pressing every single physical nerve she hadn't even known she had?

"Maybe he'll share with Matthew," the countess said. "Your brother has a way with all of these wayward Hawks."

The earl chuckled. "He certainly does."

Lily speedily set Lady Hawksfell's vanity table to rights. She knew little of Matthew Hawk other than that he was but one Hawk to visit the manor and find the future meant for him. Even Derek Hawk, who had arrived with a lady in tow last month, was happily settled with her and the handsome ex-chauffeur, Mosley.

"But Graham doesn't seem to take anything seriously," the countess said.

Lily bit her lip as she recalled just how intent he'd been when he'd wrung every drop of pleasure from her body last evening. He might be playing a game but he seemed dead serious about it.

"If that will be all, my lady?" she asked, dipping a curtsey.

"Hmm?" The countess turned then smiled at her. "Yes, Lily. Thank you."

Lily turned to leave the room, relief flooding her. She longed to be alone with her thoughts and worries, though that last was something she preferred not to consider.

"I believe Graham may surprise you," the earl said as Lily walked toward the door.

"Perhaps." The countess laughed softly. "Although I can't help hoping that yet another Hawk won't steal away more of our staff."

A chill passed through Lily. She stepped into the corridor and slumped against the wall, safely out of sight of the earl and his wife. The countess's words echoed in her head. *Steal more of the staff?* Yes, Matthew Hawk married Posy, and Patrick Hawk wed Mary, Lily's predecessor. Could the countess know what she'd done with the newest Hawk, though? With his good friend?

"Game or no, this has to stop," she muttered.

"What's that, Lily?" Cabot stepped toward her, his head cocked to the side. "What game are you playing?"

"Nothing, Cabot."

His eyes ran over her but she didn't see his usual brand of suggestiveness. No, today he looked almost contrite.

"I'm sorry about the other day," he said.

She recalled the bit of teasing he'd done out by the carriage house. She'd been terrified, but it really had nothing to do with Cabot. No. Her mind had gone back to the night the old baron forced himself on her. Besides, the pinches and grasps Cabot attempted were nothing when compared to what Graham had later done to her. Of course, she'd wanted every naughty thing he'd done and nothing of what Cabot had played at.

"It's all right," she assured him.

She could see the relief flood Cabot's face. His fair brows drew together. "Was Lord Weston harsh with you, too?"

"Harsh?" She thought of Graham's face, first as he'd taken her and then last night as he'd buried his face in her pussy. "No." Swallowing, she fought to keep her features even. "Not harsh, precisely."

Cabot pressed a hand to his chest. "Good. I was worried about you. I know how Hawks can be."

The chill from outside seemed to seep into her chest. "What do you mean?"

"I shouldn't say."

She grabbed Cabot by the lapel of his jacket and pulled him into the nearest empty room. "Tell me," she pleaded.

"You weren't here before, Lily. You don't know."

She thought for a moment. "I know the earl was different before his marriage. From what little the other staff would tell me, of course."

"And it's true. When the countess and Mr. Crowley came to the manor, things changed drastically."

She shouldn't ask but she had to know. She'd tried to get it out of Posy and then with Miss Holbrook, the lady Derek Hawk married. Neither woman would say a word about it, though. "What was it like, Cabot?"

His cheeks red, he leaned close. "He took his pleasure with the staff. Whenever and wherever he desired."

Her mouth dropped open. She'd imagined such a thing, but to hear it aloud? "You, too?"

"I...pleased him, yes."

"And *all* the staff...?"

"Not Mr. Carstairs or Mrs. Holmes, of course. But yes, all of the staff was at his disposal."

Her mind raced and she held up a hand to the wall to steady herself. "T–the other Hawks. The ones who came after. Did they...?"

Cabot shrugged. "Not to my knowledge, though there were some high jinx about the manor before each of them settled down."

"High jinx?" Her throat grew tight. "All of them?"

"Yes." Cabot's eyes widened. "Oh, I don't mean to say that Lord Weston is about any nefarious doings, Lily."

She closed her eyes. "No. I know."

"I must go see to their dinner dress."

With that, Cabot left her alone to consider what he'd told her. All of the other Hawks indulged at the manor? She'd known Posy and Matthew Hawk had been about something before he declared himself. As for Derek Hawk, she didn't have much contact with him or his new wife, Diana. They took Mosley with them, though. Did the pretty ex-chauffeur love them both? Did Diana love them?

It was astounding to think of the strange tale Cabot told. He'd pleased the earl, he'd said. Her skin flushed. Had he sucked the earl's cock as she'd sucked Graham's? That brought another possibility to her now-fertile mind. Did Colin and Graham please each other as expertly as they'd pleased her?

They were both so beautiful. Maybe the next time they were together...

"No!" she cried. She covered her mouth, praying no one had heard her outburst. "There will be no next time," she vowed, her voice lowered. "They can simply play their game without me."

Her eyes stung, but she wouldn't shed a tear. What good was crying over something that never was? Over something that could never be?

The old baron might have used her once, but she wouldn't be a plaything again.

* * * *

Colin wandered around the manor the next afternoon, with little to occupy himself. After another strange yet cozy breakfast with Graham and his new family, he felt the itch to get out and do some thinking. He and Graham hadn't talked of anything but the perfection that was Lily's mouth and pussy, and he felt a constant hum of desire whenever he thought of how beautiful she'd looked with her mouth tight on Graham's cock.

He'd almost felt every pull of her sweet suction himself then and now he couldn't wait to experience it for real. He could imagine her taste. Graham had looked supremely entranced when he'd licked her. He knew she was hot and tight, though. Colin had never felt such a tight pussy in his life. When he'd gripped her slender hips and pounded inside her, he'd felt like he could lose himself. He let himself really go for the first time since that night with Graham.

Now he wanted her mouth on his cock, and as soon as possible. Maybe he could lick her at the same time. God, maybe she could stretch out on top of him while Graham slowly fucked her.

"May I help you, Mr. Spencer?"

The question drew him up short. Mrs. Holmes voice dragged him back from his mind's illicit wanderings. Under the housekeeper's pointed gaze, Colin felt his face heat.

"Good day, Mrs. Holmes."

She clasped her hands at her waist and smiled. "Good day. Were you in need of something?"

He looked about and realized he'd come downstairs toward the kitchen. Flashing a smile at the housekeeper, he shrugged. "I'd hoped to find a bit of something to eat, I'm afraid. At Spencer House my cook always indulges my tastes."

"Lord Hawksfell and Lord Weston have gone shooting along with Mr. Crowley and will eat in the field, Mr. Spencer. Perhaps you would like a bit of something in the dining room with the countess?"

Colin shook his head. He knew Graham was busy with his new relatives, but the last thing he needed was to sit across from their hostess and make small talk when all he really wanted to do was ask her just where, precisely, her lady's maid was.

"A sandwich would be lovely, Mrs. Holmes. Perhaps something I could take up to my room?"

Her eyes widened a fraction. "Your room?"

"I'm a bit provincial, I'm afraid."

Mrs. Holmes smiled. "Not at all, Mr. Spencer. I'll have Cabot bring something up to you."

He inclined his head. "That would be wonderful, thank you." He managed to glance into what he guessed was the common room. There was no one sitting at the long table, though. Where was Lily? "Oh, do you think that maid is finished with my mending?" he asked Mrs. Holmes.

The woman blinked. "Lily? I imagine so. She's quite skilled with a needle."

And not too bad with her mouth. Colin cleared his throat as his body stiffened. "Then please send her up when she gets a moment." He smiled. "I'd like to personally thank her."

Her eyes narrowed then she nodded again. Colin climbed up the stairs to the main floor. He doubted Mrs. Holmes thought Colin wanted anything more than his mended clothes returned. He wasn't a Hawk after all, eager to fuck any and every servant he could get a hold of. He'd heard that the woman had raised the earl in the absence of his mother and that she took a shine to each and every Hawk to grace the manor in the time since Lord Hawksfell's wedding. He, however, was merely a hungry guest with an unfortunate propensity to tear his clothing.

Grinning, he climbed up to his guest room to await his lunch.

And Lily.

To his surprised delight, Graham was waiting inside.

"Graham, what are you doing here? I thought you were out shooting with the earl?"

"I was. I found I couldn't concentrate on the partridge, however. I couldn't stop thinking about Lily." He loosened his tie and leaned back. "And you."

Colin felt a smile curve his lips. "I asked to have her sent up here this afternoon."

Graham blinked his dark Hawk eyes. "Truly?" He grinned. "Well played, Colin."

Colin shrugged away his words and sank into the chair next to the hearth. He was starting to think of this liaison as less of a game and more of…something else. A knock came at the door but when Graham pulled open the door it wasn't Lily standing there. No, it was Cabot bearing a tray.

"My lord!" He bowed his head to Graham and faced Cabot. "Your sandwiches, Mr. Spencer." The footman left the tray on the dressing table.

"Thank you, Cabot," Colin said.

The footman left them and Graham grabbed one sandwich off the tray. He took a bite and chewed.

"So when is our pretty Lily coming up?" he asked.

Colin smiled. "Any moment, I wager."

Chapter 8

Lily stood outside the blue room again, Colin's clothes held carefully in her outstretched arms. She'd put off this errand as long as she could, but it wouldn't do for Mrs. Holmes to get suspicious of her intentions. Well, Graham and Colin's intentions really. Hers were to firmly refuse to play with them and to act like the fine lady's maid she was. Her conviction slipped as she rapped on the door and Colin bade her to enter. Even his voice sent shivers skittering over her skin. When she stepped into the room, the sight of him did more than that.

He looked delicious in his shirtsleeves. His trousers draped lovingly over his long legs. "Hello, Mr. Spencer."

He arched a black brow and ushered her into the room. "Ah, Lily. We are on a first-name basis, are we not?"

She gave a shaky nod and held out the clothing to him. "Your mending…Colin."

He took them from her, his fingers warm as they brushed over her chilled ones. "Thank you, love."

Then she saw that Graham was also in the room. How could she have missed him, lounging beside the fireplace? He looked delectable in his tweeds, but when he stood and began to disrobe she found herself eager to see him.

"Lock the door, Colin," Graham said, unbuttoning his shirt. "Our game must not be disturbed."

His words were like a splash of icy water. Backing toward the door, she shook her head. "I'm not a plaything."

Colin's eyes went wide, and he grabbed her hands. "No, you're not. Ah, God, we made you feel like… Damn it."

Graham stood, his dark eyes clouded. "Lily."

"I know this is just a game to you both," she managed to say.

Graham had the grace to bow his head in agreement. "That may be true, but it doesn't have to follow that you're just a plaything."

Something like hope blossomed in her chest. "What am I, then?"

Colin kissed each of her hands, his lips soft on her skin. "You're the only one we're playing with, love. Maybe I don't know all the rules, but do we need to?"

Graham was stroking the sensitive skin at the back of her neck while Colin rubbed his thumbs over her palms. Her body awoke, her nipples aching for their touch as her pussy wept. In the next instant she had a radical change of thought. Game or no, she wanted to play with the two of them.

"I may never rise from this fall," she said on a breath. "But I want you both."

Something crossed Graham's face, something like alarm. Then his eyes glinted in that now-familiar way. "Oh, we'll take you. Both of us."

Colin removed her blouse and unfastened her corset. "I want to taste you, Lily." He flicked his tongue over the breasts he revealed. "And I want you to taste me."

Her mouth watered at the prospect. Graham's taste was spicy like his scent. Would Colin taste of freshness? "I want to taste you, too," she admitted on a whisper.

She soon found herself naked, stretched out on the coverlet with the two of them. Graham kissed her lips as Colin sucked and pinched her nipples. It was exquisite, feeling both of them working their particular brand of magic. It wasn't enough, though. They were each wearing only their trousers, but it was still too many clothes for her. She came up on her knees, tossing back her head and letting her loosened hair fall down her back. They both stopped, staring hard at her.

"My God, you're incredible," Colin breathed.

Graham nodded slowly. "Like a goddess."

"A goddess?" She couldn't help but smile. "I rather like that."

"Command us, dear goddess," Colin said, his voice low.

She ran her eyes over their impressive chests and flat, ridged stomachs. They each bulged in the front of their trousers and that surge of power she'd felt yesterday filled her again. "Disrobe, my servants."

Graham barked out a laugh as he tore at his pants. Colin was soon naked as well, and she gasped as she looked at both of their cocks. Both were long and thick, and topped with broad heads. They'd each been inside her, too. Every ridge exquisitely driving her to climax. Today their cocks boasted a drop of pearly liquid she longed to taste.

"What do you think, goddess?" Graham asked, giving his cock a long, slow stroke.

She licked her lips. "It looks bigger than yesterday."

Colin sat back on his heels, his cock held before him. "What of mine?"

She let her gaze run over his shaft. "You felt huge in my pussy, but now…"

"Touch me," Colin said.

"Suck him," Graham said. "Colin, you have to feel the perfection of Lily's mouth on your cock."

Her mouth watered for a taste of Colin today. Lowering her mouth, she gave the head of his cock a slow lick.

"Christ," Colin bit out, falling back on the bed.

She glanced at Graham, who was watching her intently as he stroked himself. Grasping Colin's cock with both hands, she engulfed the head. Colin arched, his hips flexing as he moved. She felt his hands on her waist, and the next moment she found herself straddling his face.

"Colin!"

His fingers held her open and in place as he began to lick her. It was divine, and she wriggled over his magical mouth. Pleasure was coiling within her so quickly she almost lost her breath. She had to brace her hands on either side of Colin's narrow hips to hold herself up, but she wouldn't release his cock from her mouth. His taste was everything she'd imagined, and his cock was every bit as impressive in her mouth as Graham's had been. Writhing, she gave herself over to this man. That was, until she felt Graham's hands on her bottom.

"Do you like this, Lily?" Graham asked her.

She gave a small nod, earning a groan from Colin. Increasing her suction, she surged toward climax herself. Graham dipped a finger between her bottom then, shocking her. She lifted her head to glance at him over her shoulder.

"Graham, what are you doing?" she asked on a soft moan.

He smiled at her and held up a small jar. "Cream will ease my way, love, but I have to fuck your ass."

She gasped, and then Colin grabbed on to her thighs, high up near her bottom, and held her as he devoured her. Closing her eyes, she arched into the feeling.

"May I, goddess?" Graham asked, all traces of teasing gone from his voice now.

He had two fingers in her bottom now, moving and stretching her. Would his cock fit inside her...there? The head of his cock began to tease her hole as Colin kept up his delightful torture.

"Y–yes..." She braced herself as he slowly entered her. She felt tight and full and she wanted more. "Graham!"

"I'm in!" Graham cursed long and low. "Hot and tight."

"Like her pussy," Colin said, his voice thick. "Suck me, Lily."

She renewed her attention to Colin's cock, pouring everything they were making her feel into her efforts. He shuddered beneath her, groaning as he lifted his hips. The next moment he came, flooding her mouth with his taste as Graham had done yesterday. He was as delicious, too. She didn't have the chance to revel much in it as he now drove two fingers deep in her pussy as Graham moved in and out of her bottom.

"Oh!" She struggled to hold herself up as they worked her. Graham was moving hard and fast now, Colin's fingers moving in concert as he nibbled on her clit.

"Come, Lily," Graham said, his voice strained. "God, I'm going to come!"

He did, and she came hard against Colin's mouth. Her orgasm went on forever, her shouts of ecstasy reverberating in her head as they each held her.

Afterward they collapsed, shifting until they flanked her.

"In your ass," Graham said, holding her close. "Astoundingly sweet, goddess."

She hid her smile against his chest. "I never imagined."

"You drenched me," Colin said. "You're like nectar, love."

Lifting her head, she met his gaze. "I've never felt anything like what the two of you did." She looked at Graham. "I don't know what to say."

"Say nothing, then," Graham said, holding her close. "You don't have to say a thing."

Colin murmured his agreement, stroking his fingers through her hair. She found herself wanting to tell them more, though. That they made her forget that horrible night before she left the old baron. That they made her feel strong and desirable and...*right* for wanting them to do what they did. She did want it in the heat of the moment. She wanted it still in the aftermath.

She only hoped she could live without it when they left Hawksfell Manor.

* * * *

"Tell me what frightened you the other day, love," Graham asked.

He felt Lily go still against his chest.

"I don't know what you're talking about," she finally said.

He and Colin exchanged a look. They'd spent themselves in her delectable form, and he was amazed to find himself wanting her again. That wasn't why he wanted her to open up to him, though. Hell, he didn't know why he wanted that, but he craved a connection to her like he had with Colin.

"The other afternoon, Lily." Graham cupped her cheek, feeling its smoothness with his thumb. "When I came upon you and Cabot."

"I told you. He was teasing, is all."

"Graham said you looked frightened." Colin leaned up on one elbow, his brow knit. "After what we just shared, don't you know you can trust us?"

She gathered the sheets to her bosom, her eyes large. "I can trust you?"

Graham placed a hand on his chest. "I swear, I won't divulge anything to anyone. Not the earl and not the servants."

She nibbled that delectable lower lip of hers and eyed Colin. "Do you swear, too?"

"On my honor," Colin said.

She took in a breath and slowly let it out. What the devil was she going to say? In that instant, Graham wasn't certain he wanted to know.

"At my last position, my employer…" Her gaze slid from them to settle in the vicinity of the fireplace. "He wasn't a nice man."

Anger burned in Graham's belly. "He forced you."

Squeezing her eyes shut, she nodded. "He did."

"Who was it?" Colin asked.

She shook her head. "It doesn't matter, does it?"

"We can expose him," Colin added.

"No, we can't," Graham said. "He was a noble, yes?" At her nod, he went on. "There's little a servant can do in that situation. Believe me, I've gleaned a bit of information of the previous generation of Hawks. From the earl's father to Matthew Hawk's uncle, a noble can hold power over his servants with little recourse."

"Bastard," Colin said.

Graham found a smile. "Yes well, not all of us are legitimate."

Colin chuckled, catching his intent to lighten the mood a bit. "When was this, Lily?" he asked.

She straightened her shoulders. "Before I came here. I admit the glowing recommendation the old baron wrote me might have been a bit…forced as well."

"Ha! Good for the rutting lout," Graham said. He grabbed a gentle hold of her and urged her to rest between them once again. "Was he your first?"

"My only." She ducked her head but he saw she blushed prettily. "Until you two, that is."

Something shifted in Graham's chest at her admission. He was her first after what had happened to her? His heart began to race. He searched his mind at a lightning pace. Was he much different than that "old baron," really? He hadn't forced her, no. Yet he'd used every tool in his blasted Hawk bag of tricks to seduce her.

"I'm sorry," he muttered.

"For what?" she asked.

"I should never have…" He held out his hands. "I should have known you weren't experienced."

"How?" she asked.

"You're very small, Lily," Colin said. He winked. "And hot and tight and wet."

"Colin!" She laughed a bit, losing that haunted expression in her eyes. "This is so strange," she went on. "I don't know quite what this is."

Graham had to find some steadier footing and fast. He had no idea what this was among them, and he wasn't going to sit here trying to figure it out. Not with the two of them still within reach. "Let's not worry about that now, love."

Colin blinked then offered her a smile. "Graham's right. Sometimes trying to put a name on something can prove too stifling."

As Lily seemed to accept Colin's assertions, Graham's gut twisted again. Here he was, naked and spent with two people he wanted more than any others he'd ever encountered, and he was eager to quit the room before there was any possibility that talk would turn to hearts and flowers.

He took the avenue Colin paved for him and didn't say anything more about just what, precisely, this was among the three of them.

But damn him to hell, he couldn't wait to be with them both again and soon.

Chapter 9

The next afternoon Lily found herself at Colin's door again. She'd tried to stay away, especially after confiding her awful secret to him and Graham. Neither seemed to judge her, however. She thought back to when Posy had still been a maid here. Her reputation had dogged her heels so fiercely that Lily had known of it despite the months passed since the earl's wedding. A glimmer of hope flickered just out of reach. If Posy was able to set aside those rumors and secure the loves of her life, was there a chance for Lily?

"I'm not going to be a viscountess," she chided herself. Graham might not wish to discuss what this all was, but she knew. She was a plaything, though a willing one this time. He and Colin knew just what she wanted and she wasn't going to worry about it now.

Taking a breath, she raised her hand to rap lightly on the door.

"Back for more, sweet Lily?" Graham asked, his mouth close to her ear.

She spun to find him looming over her. His scent surrounded her and his heat was evident. He only wore his shirt and tweed trousers, and he looked remarkable.

"Graham," she gasped.

He smiled. "Looking to get fucked, love?"

Her mouth dropped open. His words should have shocked her, and in a way they did, but there was truth there. *Two could play this game.* She almost giggled. *Three, actually.*

Schooling her expression, she lifted her chin. "I want you both, yes."

Heat flared in his dark eyes, and he reached around her to grasp the doorknob. His lips grazed her cheek and she shivered. When the door opened behind her, she fell back into Colin's arms.

"What a lovely surprise," he murmured, bringing his lips to the sensitive skin at the nape of her neck.

Graham closed the door with an audible click as Colin turned her to face him. He began to kiss and caress her. His tongue was in her mouth, and she reached up on her toes and angled her head to take all of him. That now-familiar need swirled through her as Colin held her closer still.

"She wants us both, Colin." Graham brushed behind her to stand behind Colin. He reached both hands around Colin's narrow waist and cupped her bottom. She lifted her head to give Graham her mouth now. Oh, their tastes mingled and her mouth watered.

"Mmm." Graham urged her toward him, bringing her flush against Colin's long, hard cock. "Does she know I want the both of you as well?"

Her breath caught and she broke away from the kiss. She looked up at Colin and saw heat in his sparkling blue eyes. "Both?" she asked, not caring a whit which man answered her.

Was that uncertainty in Colin's eyes as he glanced at Graham? His dear face showed furrows in his brow that cleared in the next moment. "Graham?"

Graham growled behind him, bringing his face to Colin's neck and nipping him. Colin shivered and Lily felt it as though she was the one with Graham's hard body pressed against her.

"I want to fuck you, Colin," he said.

Lily gasped, her pussy swelling as she imagined the two of them intertwined. "Truly?"

Graham chuckled and caught her eye even as Colin leaned back in obvious surrender. "You want to watch, don't you love?"

"Y–yes," she said.

Colin snapped to attention and began to tear at his clothes. Graham stripped and made quick work of her garments, too. "I want to see you flushed and pretty as I love Colin."

She could only nod. As Graham swiftly removed her clothes and underthings, running eager hands over her flesh until she tingled, she studied Colin's body. He was just beautiful, all smooth muscles and hard planes like a statue. His cock strained toward her, and she grasped him.

Graham stepped behind Colin again and stroked his chest. Lily flicked her tongue over Colin's flat little nipples, earning a moan from him between her and Graham. He gasped, and she knew what Graham did to him. She'd felt that particular sensation when he'd fingered her hole. When he'd pushed inside of her. Would he take Colin that way now?

"Easy, Colin," Graham said, his voice strained. "I'm going to burst if I don't get inside you."

"Take me, Graham," Colin said, arching toward him.

Lily's body flushed just as Graham had predicted. She stepped back and watched as Graham sank into Colin. Colin reached up to wrap an arm around Graham's neck as the two of them began to move in rhythm. She was dripping wet now, her every cell primed as though she was the one being loved by Graham. Colin bit his full lower lip and Lily mimicked the motion.

"Oh, you're both so beautiful!" she cried.

Graham glanced in her direction. "Suck him, love." He groaned and increased his thrusts. "Suck Colin's cock."

She didn't need any further instructions. A drop of liquid glistened on the tiny slit on the head of Colin's cock, so tempting to her. Falling to her knees, she took Colin deep down her throat. He trembled, bracing his legs apart as he cupped her head with an incredibly gentle touch.

"Sweet Lily," he breathed. "Oh, Graham!"

She knew he was about to come. He quaked between them. Taking all of him, she grabbed onto his taut buttocks. Graham covered her hands with his, and the two of them did their best to drive

Colin over the edge. Colin moaned long and loud as he filled her mouth. She tasted his cream as Graham shouted out his climax behind him.

Sitting back on her heels, she tried to catch her breath. Colin turned his head and kissed Graham. It nearly sent her over the edge.

"Oh, someone must take me!" she gasped.

Graham chuckled, apparently a bit out of breath himself, and shook his head. "I'm afraid there must be a delay, Lily. We're both spent."

"Spent?" Colin swore softly as they both disengaged. "I was nearly turned inside out by the two of you."

She came up on her knees, cupping her breasts and pinching her nipples. Her body was on fire and she needed the release she knew they could give her. "Please…"

Graham's eyes all but crackled. He grabbed her ankles and pulled her down on the carpet. His mouth claimed her pussy, his tongue stabbing into her as he held her thighs far apart.

"Oh, yes!" She tossed her head from side to side, eager for everything he was doing to her. Colin's mouth closed over one of her nipples, and that was all she needed. Her climax roared through her as she writhed helplessly on the floor. Pinned by Graham's strong hands, her pussy convulsed and her clit throbbed as wave after wave of pleasure left her gasping.

Graham finally released her, and Colin cuddled her close.

"Look at that pretty, pink pussy, Colin," Graham said. "We'll have to fill it and soon."

She blushed as she smiled, which amazed her. She was still spread wide before the two of them. Then Graham's odd wording struck her. "Soon?"

"I won't be at the manor much longer," he said.

Colin helped her to her feet and kissed her, brushing her hair from her eyes. "And I suppose I'll have to get back to Spencer House."

If she wasn't mistaken, they both wore expressions of regret.

Well, she wouldn't flatter herself to think they'd never shared such things with another woman between them. They were far too virile to be as inexperienced as she was.

She couldn't ask the question burning within her, though. Neither of them were in need of a lady's maid, and she wasn't going to be mistress to them either.

Without another word, she dressed quickly and left them. Thankfully no one was about when she reached her attic room. It was then and only then that she let the tears fall. She cried for the intense pleasure they gave her and for the incredible tenderness they showed.

As for anything her own heart might be feeling? She would just ignore it and hope that no one at the manor ever learned of her indiscretion with the earl's latest relative and his good friend. She would never be so lucky as to get the countess to write any sort of recommendation should this be the reason for her termination.

* * * *

Colin stared at the closed door after Lily left them. "That was surprising."

Graham pulled on his trouser and ran a hand through his hair. "I wanted you, Colin. I wanted her to love you, too."

Colin's stomach dipped as he turned to face his friend. "You love me, Graham?"

Graham's gaze skittered away, though. "You're the closest thing I have to family, you know. The earl and the other Hawks aside."

Colin knew he shouldn't say it, not right at the moment, but he had to anyway. "I love you, too."

He held his breath, but Graham only gave a jerky nod. "Look, I don't know how to do this."

Colin held up a hand. "I'm not asking you to decide our future, for God's sake."

Graham finally met his gaze. His dark eyes almost looked

haunted, and Colin fought the urge to wrap his arms around him.

"I want you both," Graham said. "And I don't know how the hell this happened."

Colin swallowed his own conflicted feelings and dressed. "I think I should go back to Spencer House."

"Just like you told Lily?"

Colin shrugged. "It seemed like the thing to say at the time. She looked so hurt, though. That, I hadn't expected."

"You heard her tale, Colin. Her last employer raped her, for God's sake! And we just took her. Over and over. No doubt she feels like she doesn't matter."

"She matters to me." The words startled Colin as he said them. They felt right, though. True. "She's beautiful and sweet, and she's our match sexually. Now I doubt we'll get to both love her."

"I know. She's become more than a diversion, that's true."

"More than a game?" Colin had to know.

Graham shrugged. "I don't want to see her hurt, actually. Any more than I'd want to see you injured. Hell, I want to keep her safe. That was never part of the game I'd planned in my mind. Is that love, do you think?"

Colin found a smile. They might not have the answers, but at least they were talking open and honestly, like they always had. "How the hell would I know if that's love?"

Graham chuckled. "I have to figure this all out, though. Gabriel said we can stay as long as we like."

"You, Graham. *You* can stay. You're his family."

"He extended the invitation to you." Graham looked pensive for a moment. "You know, I think he suspects we're closer than friends."

Colin's heart jumped a beat. "Are we?"

Graham met his gaze. "I fucked you, Colin. You've pleased me before, and I fucked you."

"So what? Isn't that what happened at Spencer House the night before we came here?"

Graham groaned. "Please don't remind me."

"What?" Colin could hardly believe his ears. Any hope he had for some sort of future seemed far out of reach. "You regret that night," he muttered.

"God, no! I am making a mess of this." Graham's eyes were so serious, something he'd rarely seen. "That night felt so different from anything I've ever encountered, Colin. I didn't want it to change our friendship."

"Ah." Colin let out a breath. "So you decided to pretend it never happened."

"I suppose. I couldn't manage that, though. And now that we've added Lily to the mix…"

He caught Colin's gaze, and he felt an echo of the pleasure Graham and Lily had given him.

"She's a perfect fit," Colin said.

Graham stared at him for a beat. "For what?"

Colin thought for a moment, and then he knew. "For us."

Graham just shook his head, uncertainty clear on his face. Well, Colin wouldn't be the one to smack some sense into his Hawk mind. It was up to him to decide what future he wanted.

As for Colin, he knew. He wanted a life with both Graham and Lily in it.

Chapter 10

Cabot put the finishing touches on Graham's dinner dress that evening, keeping his eyes downcast.

"You know, you don't have to feel badly for wanting her," Graham said.

Cabot lifted his head to face him. "My lord, I don't know what you're talking about."

"You don't, hmm?" Graham arched a brow. "Seems to me that what I saw you attempting out by the garage was quite clear. Have you forgotten?"

Cabot placed Graham's things on the dressing table, then turned to face him. "I've apologized to her, my lord. It was never my intention to frighten her." Regret was in all his looks, and Graham knew the footman spoke the truth. "She's just so bloody beautiful." His eyes went wide. "Forgive me for plain speaking!"

Graham shook his head. "No reason for forgiveness. Not on my part. Not for your language nor for the sentiment. She is the prettiest girl I've ever encountered."

"She's a good girl, Lord Weston. She might be lovely to look at, but she's never…" Cabot swallowed. "She wasn't here before the earl wed."

Whispers of the gossip Colin had shared came back to him. Gossip which Gabriel confirmed, actually. "What do you mean?"

"She was never a part of that business."

Cabot looked expectantly at him, and Graham nodded. "Thank you, Cabot. You may go see to Mr. Spencer."

Cabot bowed and left. Graham had known that about Lily, that she'd come to the manor months after Gabriel's wedding, but having the footman say it made him feel better somehow. Like she'd been waiting for him and Colin to make her theirs.

"What the hell am I going to do?" he asked himself.

He went downstairs to wait for dinner with the earl and his family. It was clear that Colin was smitten with the girl. More than smitten, if Graham didn't miss his guess.

"And he loves me," he marveled aloud.

"What's that, cousin?" Matthew Hawk asked.

"N–nothing," he answered.

Matthew laughed softly, coming to stand close to him. "I've seen that expression before, Graham. In the mirror, actually."

Graham thought for a moment. This was a man who obviously loved his wife. That lady, Posy the former parlor maid, was nearby as well. Her pretty little face with its large blue eyes sparkled as she swatted Matthew's arm.

"Do not tease Graham," Posy said. She looked over at the countess. "Millicent, do tell Matthew to play nice."

"Matthew is your concern, Posy," the countess said with a smile. "As for Graham…" She tilted her head to the side, considering him for a long moment. "*Are* you playing, Graham?" she finally asked.

Graham stilled. She couldn't know about his original intentions when he first came to Hawksfell Manor. His first match had been with Lily, which had effectively put an end to any game-playing with the staff on his part.

"I'm just awaiting dinner, Millicent," he assured her with a smile.

She quirked him a look. "Of course."

"Good evening," Colin said, joining them.

"Hello," the earl said. "We're apparently discussing games, Colin."

Graham flinched as Colin paled a bit. His eyes sought Graham's. He nodded at Colin, a gesture he didn't much care if the others intercepted. It was a friendly nod of greeting, really. When Colin's eyes warmed, Graham felt it like an embrace. *Colin loved him.*

The dinner gong rang, and they went in to eat. After, when the Hawks and Colin separated from the ladies, Matthew came up to him again.

"What is this 'game' business, Graham?" he asked.

"It's nothing."

"You went all red, and when Colin joined us he went all white. There's something going on."

He saw that Colin was speaking to the earl, so he bent his head to Matthew's. "I've taken up with one of the maids."

Matthew blinked then nodded. "Ah. And you're just playing and she wants an arrangement."

"No," Graham countered softly.

Matthew quirked a brow. "No about the game or no about the arrangement?"

"Both, actually," he admitted.

"What of..." He tossed his head in Colin's direction. "I know you're quite close."

Graham studied Colin where he stood with the earl. He was so handsome, so earnest. He was such a good man and a great friend, and Graham couldn't consider his life going forward without him. He couldn't speak of it to Matthew, though.

"It's like that," Matthew said.

Graham searched his cousin's face. Knowledge showed in his eyes, and for the first time Graham felt a kinship toward one of these Hawks. "I..."

"With Posy and me..." Matthew interjected with a smile. "I don't suppose you know of William?"

"The footman?"

"First footman, actually. And only because he insists on bringing something to our union."

Graham suspected an arrangement among the earl and his wife and her third cousin, but was such a thing going on in Matthew's marriage as well? "Your union. You and Posy…and William?"

Matthew gave a slow nod. "I'm not the first Hawk to break his curse with two loves. You have but to look at my brother to see the evidence of that."

"I guess I have seen the evidence. I just didn't want to believe it."

"Come now, Graham. You're a Hawk. You fuck everything just like the rest of us."

Graham offered Matthew a small smile. "I didn't mean that. Of course I know our urges can take us anywhere for release. But for love? I just don't believe it."

"What are you two talking about?" Millicent walked up to them.

Graham hadn't noticed that the women had joined the men in the drawing room up to that moment. Gabriel's wife looked to be hiding a smile as she took Graham's arm.

"Matthew has been bending your ear about something, Graham," she said. "And what is that guilty expression on your handsome Hawk face?"

Graham felt his cheeks heat. "Guilty?"

"Hmm." She tilted her head as she had earlier. "Never say you're going to take away more of my staff."

"Millicent!" Matthew said. "How can you talk of this here?"

"Pretty words, Matthew." She winked. "Did you or did you not take my favorite parlormaid?"

"Hardly your favorite," Posy said, coming to stand beside them as well. "Besides, Matthew is far from being the only Hawk to…" Matthew's wife shrugged her slight shoulders.

"The only Hawk to steal away a member of our staff? Hardly. I've yet to find a chauffeur as capable as Mosley," Gabriel put in from where he stood with Colin. "Colin, tell me you're not with him in this endeavor."

Colin met Graham's eyes as his cheeks turned pink. He faced Gabriel. "I don't know what you're speaking of, Lord Hawksfell."

The earl laughed and clapped Colin on the back. "Of course not."

Graham found himself grinning now. This was passing strange, and not only because the conversation was so inappropriate. To joke with family was an oddity for him. With a pang, he realized he would miss it when his visit ended.

"So your chauffeur…?" he began in question.

"Is now with our cousin Derek Hawk, I'm afraid." Gabriel's dark eyes sparkled. "He and his wife cannot do without him."

"Ah, his wife," The countess's third cousin Michael Crowley put in. "I believe she is Derek's third cousin, isn't that so Millie?"

The countess clicked her tongue, but affection was clear in her blue gaze. "Yes, Michael."

"And you only have to speak to Gabriel's man-of-affairs Grantley to know the truth of his particular arrangement," Michael continued.

"Ah, but Grantley is as silent as a tomb," Matthew quipped. "I daresay dear Millicent lost another fine maid with that business."

"Business of the heart though, Matthew," Posy said, her voice going soft. "Mary deserves everything she has."

Matthew bent his head to Posy's, their brows touching. "She's not the only one."

Suddenly Graham felt like an intruder once again. These Hawks had found their loves. True, he had Colin. If they continued to be lovers, he would thank his blighted Hawk stars. As to continuing on as they'd been, though? Taking nameless, faceless women together for a night's pleasure? The thought caused his belly to clench.

After loving Lily, he couldn't imagine a better match for the two of them.

* * * *

"So what was that about?" Colin asked Graham the next morning.

"What?" Graham shouldered his rifle and fell into step beside him.

The day was bright, and the chill of November all but forgotten as

Colin and he joined the others for shooting. The participants were scattered far and wide over the earl's wooded section of property, so he reasoned he wouldn't get a better chance than now to discuss this with Graham.

All night he'd tried to make sense of what the others were talking about after dinner, but could only glean that there was more to every union than he first presumed.

"That oddly candid discussion in the drawing room with your relatives," Colin said. "I know you and I talked about the earl and his wife."

"And her cousin," Graham put in. "Michael Crowley appears to be as much a part of that union as Gabriel."

"Is it possible, do you think?"

"What are you asking? You and I have shared numerous women over the years, Colin."

"I'm not talking about the fucking."

Graham narrowed his eyes. "Are you saying you would welcome an arrangement like theirs?"

Colin looked at the ground as they continued through the woods. "I would welcome love, Graham. It's all I've ever wanted."

Graham took his elbow and turned him. "I don't know if I can do forever, Colin." His dark eyes looked haunted. "I never knew my mother or father. The other Hawks have known only neglect from their parents or, in Matthew's case, abuse. If we continue on as we've been, there may be more to consider than if the girl cares for us or not."

"You mean children?"

"We've both spilled our seed in her delectable body. Something is bound to take root if this continues. As I said, Lily's feelings may be immaterial."

Cold settled in Colin's belly. "Can you truly not see that the girl is in love with you?"

"What?"

"She was innocent, Graham. She was raped, but before your time with her in the garage she was, in effect, a virgin."

"You really believe she loves me?"

Colin screwed up his courage and placed a hand on Graham's shoulder. "How could she not?"

Affection, pure and sweet, filled Graham's eyes then. "Then you must allow that she loves you, too."

"Of course." Colin grinned. "The question is, can you name the moment when this all ceased to be a game?"

"It's not my game any longer." Graham laughed as they turned to join the others on the trek back to the house. Their footfalls crunched over the crisp, cold leaves.

"You know," Graham said after a while. "Matthew's wife was a maid."

Colin stopped in his tracks. His heart began to race. Was Graham saying what he thought he was? "And?" he asked him.

Graham shrugged, his brows drawn together. "Patrick Hawk's, as well."

His heart began to beat a more normal tempo. "And?" Colin prodded again. "Are you suggesting marriage?"

"Why not?"

Colin studied him for a long moment then shook his head. "You had better come up with a better proposal than that."

"Do you think she would accept us?"

Colin stared at him for a beat. "Us?"

"Colin, I love you. You would have to be a part of this. An equal part."

Colin covered his heart with his hand. "I don't know what to say."

"Say that we can figure out some way to get the girl to realize she's more to us than a plaything."

Colin thought for a moment. "We haven't taken her together yet."

Graham stilled. "She took me in her pretty little ass, Colin. You tasted how wet she was when I did that."

Colin sucked in a breath. "I can just imagine how her pussy will feel around my cock when you fuck her ass again."

"If that doesn't prove she's important to the both of us, to our pleasure and our happiness, then damn me for a fool."

Colin threw his arm around Graham's shoulder. "No one would ever call you a fool, friend."

Chapter 11

Lily sat in her lonely room in the attic, wishing she could be anywhere but here at the manor. There was nowhere else, though. She was never going to find a better position. She'd known that upon securing employment here. She'd traded her hard-won security for a moment's pleasure. First with Graham and then with Colin, she'd surrendered. She'd thrown everything away in pursuit of lust. That was all it was, of course. Lust and a shared desire among the three of them.

Oh, what they'd shared yesterday! Loving Colin together only strengthened her need for Graham as well, as impossible as that should be. Tasting Colin's release and finding her own with Graham's skillful tongue was something she could never have imagined before their liaison began. She'd been on fire for completion after Graham had taken Colin. After she'd sucked him so far down her throat she'd nearly consumed him. In that moment before she combusted through Graham's ministrations, she'd caught hold of one thought. She could go on feeling this way forever.

"And now you have to do without it," she whispered to herself.

Her body heated as she cuddled under the coverlet. Her hand drifted over her aching breasts to touch her pussy. She was damp beneath her nightdress. She'd never touched herself before, having never had urges when she was employed by the old baron. Certainly after his rough, unwanted treatment she'd had no notion pleasure could be achieved at all.

Nothing had made her crave a sensual touch again. Not even handsome Mosley the chauffeur had tempted her to give herself away.

Not Cabot's pretty face or clumsy hands, neither. But now that Graham and Colin had awakened her own hidden beast, she couldn't imagine living without passion. What would become of her now? She withdrew her hand and fisted it on top of the coverlet.

It was only a matter of time before the countess learned of her shame with the earl's relative and that man's friend. What would she think of her? Lady Hawksfell's good opinion was one of the shining benefits of this position in her opinion. To lose the countess's warmth and caring would surely leave a black mark on Lily's heart.

Sniffling, she squeezed her burning eyes shut. Losing Graham and Colin was a foregone conclusion. Whyever would they want to continue an arrangement with a maid, for goodness sake? She simply had to confess to Lady Hawksfell and assure her that nothing like this would ever happen again. She wasn't trying to emulate Posy's incredibly good fortune to find a Hawk to love her. Posy had not only Matthew Hawk but William as well! Before this liaison with Graham and Colin, she would have doubted such a path to bliss was possible. Now she knew far better.

She had no such illusions that her life would be anything but what she'd managed so far. This was lust, pure and simple.

She sadly shook her head. "No, not simple." She was beginning to love the both of them.

They were sweet and tender to her, when they weren't occupied with driving her out of her mind with pleasure. Their hands could be gentle even as they coaxed screams of ecstasy from her lips. Their cocks...No, she wouldn't think about their cocks. "That way lies madness," she chided herself.

Once Graham and Colin returned to their lives, she would admit to all of it. Perhaps the countess wouldn't turn her out without reference. Perhaps she would forgive her for succumbing to men far more experienced than herself.

If not, Lily was better off returning to London and finding work in a shop than attempting to work in another great house.

* * * *

Long after dinner that night, Graham paced his room. He'd managed to keep his expression clear in the face of the obvious love and warmhearted jests among the Hawks and their partners. His talk with Colin in the woods made him long for things he surely had no business wanting. Then again, he'd never imagined his friendship with Colin would deepen into romantic love. He'd cared for him for so long, back when they were at school and later as they gained manhood. Maybe he'd always loved him.

Perhaps the stifling upbringing his great aunt and uncle gave him made him believe there was no real great passion where the heart was concerned. The cock, of course. He'd never denied his beast, and he never thought of being a Hawk as being cursed. That assurance, too, he could lay at Colin's feet. And now, with Lily?

Lily could be everything to them, if they were able to convince her. Colin was confident that she loved them. Graham was less sure of that fact. She didn't know of love either. From what she'd told them, love had nothing to do with what her previous employer had done. Then she'd come here to find Cabot and no doubt the other male servants drooling over her. She looked...lonely.

During tonight's particular conversation before dinner, he'd managed to bring up the subject of Lady Hawksfell's previous maids. Patrick Hawk had married the girl that preceded Lily, according to Posy. She also said that she and Lily never really had time to grow close but the countess was very happy with her service. He'd had to keep his face impassive as he thought of Lily's most recent service. Naked and on her knees in Colin's guest room.

A knock came to his door and he crossed to open it. Relief swamped him when he spied Colin in the hall. "Where is she?"

Colin pulled back then offered him a small smile. "Easy. I've called for her."

"What did Mrs. Holmes say about that?"

"Nothing." Colin shrugged. "I'm just a slightly eccentric friend to one of the Hawks, Graham. She doesn't know I share, shall I say, an accelerated libido with you and your Hawk relatives."

"Are you sure you're not a Hawk bastard, Colin?"

Colin chuckled. "Sadly, no. My parents are very much in love and always have been."

Graham acknowledged this with a nod. Colin's whole family was ridiculously happy, and that was one reason his friend preferred to stay at Spencer House without them.

"Well, when will she be here?"

"Planning to get on one knee?" Colin asked.

Graham found a smile. "Ah, I'm going to get on both tonight."

Colin's eyes sparkled, and Graham welcomed the closeness now. It wasn't stifling, like he'd feared. No, it was like a warmth wrapping around his heart.

He stepped forward and grabbed the back of Colin's head. Bringing his mouth to his, he kissed him then slapped him on the back. "Go get her, damn it."

Colin nodded and went back out into the hall. "Ah, Lily."

He heard Lily's soft reply but couldn't quite make out the words. Nevertheless, Graham felt desire lick a hot tongue down his shaft. Their girl was in the hall with Colin, and surely she knew what they really wanted when Mrs. Holmes sent her up here. She didn't know they planned to take her together, but he knew she would love it.

"Graham's room?" she asked as Colin tugged her inside.

"Yes, love," Graham answered her. He stepped forward and took her hands as Colin shut and locked the door. "Tonight we're going to take you in my bed." He shrugged. "Well, my guest bed."

She bit her lip in that adorable way she had, her green eyes luminous. "Both of you tonight?"

"Both of us, yes." Colin began to remove his clothes. "Tonight and maybe more."

Her delicate brows drew together. "More? Oh, you're not leaving the manor right away then?"

Graham and Colin exchanged a look. They wanted her forever, but now wasn't the time to talk of the particulars. They would just overwhelm her with pleasure and let their bodies speak for their hearts.

"Get out of that uniform, Lily," he said as he undressed himself. "If I lay a finger on that silky white skin of yours, I'll come before we even start."

She gasped, her gaze going to where he tented his trousers. "Graham..."

"Come here," Colin said.

He wore nothing now, and Graham admired his body for a moment before the man stripped Lily bare.

"God, look at the both of you." He cupped himself through his trousers and cursed softly. "You're going to kill me."

Colin laughed, and Lily offered a shy smile. Her body was incredible, all lush curves and silken skin. Taken with Colin's smooth muscles and broad chest, Graham nearly came at the sight.

Colin took Lily's hand and led her to the bed. "I'm going to start, Lily."

He sat up near the headboard and let her straddle his thighs. When he closed his eyes and hissed softly, Graham knew her pussy must be like heaven against his cock. They began to kiss, Lily making the most amazing sounds as Colin's hands stroked up and down her back again and again until he cupped her pert ass. Graham was going to fuck that ass tonight, as he had before. But with Colin inside her as well? That was truly going to feel like heaven.

"Colin," she sighed, letting her head fall back as Colin moved his mouth to her ample breasts.

She shivered as his mouth closed over one nipple and Graham fumbled to get the rest of his clothes off. Finally he joined them, coming behind her to run his aching cock over her round little cheeks.

Her body was already glistening with sweat, and his hands slid deliciously as they roamed over her supple thighs and slender hips as she caught Colin's rhythm.

"Ah, love," he said, nibbling on her ear. "You feel so good between us."

She murmured something and clutched at Colin's shoulders. Her every muscle was tensed with her frustration, so Graham reached down to finger her pussy. She was soaking wet, and he knew Colin would have no problem getting into her tight passage. Glancing down at his own cock, he'd never seemed bigger. He'd certainly never felt so eager in all his blighted life.

"I'm going to take your pretty bottom before Colin slides into you," he told her.

She glanced over her shoulders then, her mouth open in obvious shock. "Like before?"

He stroked her ass, his finger just outside her little hole. "Did you like that?"

She blushed pink but nodded.

"I didn't hurt you?" he had to know.

"N–no," she whispered.

He grinned and kissed her parted lips. "Good."

As Colin continued to rouse her every passion with his lips and hands, Graham opened the jar of cream he'd used last time. Two of his fingers slid into her ass, and she braced herself. "Easy," he soothed, kissing the soft skin at the back of her neck. With a groan, he pressed the tip of his cock against her hole until he began to slide inside.

"Oh, Graham," she gasped.

"Take me, Lily," he said, holding his breath as he felt her muscles ease a bit. "Let me inside. God, let me inside."

She backed toward him just a bit, but it was enough. He was inside now, holding on to her hips as he throbbed. He wanted to move but knew he had to let her get used to him like before. Taking the chance to move at last, he slid slowly back and forth and she began to tremble.

"Finger her, Colin," he bit out.

"You're soaking wet," Colin said. "I want to feel you around my cock."

"Mmm, yes!" she said, nodding frantically. "I need you inside me, too!"

Colin shifted to lower her onto his shaft. Graham felt him. It was amazing, feeling him moving as they sought a rhythm to drive her out of her mind.

"Do you feel us, Lily?" he asked, sliding in as Colin slid out. They repeated the motions, slowly building speed as she moaned softly.

"This is just... Oh, it's lovely!" she cried.

Graham closed his eyes and let himself feel these two people he loved sharing with him the most incredible experience he'd ever had. He never wanted it to end. This passion. This connection.

And if he had his way, it never would.

Chapter 12

Lily could hardly think with the two of them inside of her. She felt so full, so hot and trembling, that she couldn't do more than gasp and cry out. Colin was deep in her pussy, using his fit body to thrust upward as her clit rubbed against his pelvic bone. Graham was in her bottom, his hands gripping her as he alternately filled her and withdrew just enough to allow for Colin's upward thrusts.

Their bodies were filmed with sweat, their combined scents filling her head as surely as the two of them filled her body. Colin's face was pressed against her throat, his mouth nibbling and kissing as he grunted softly. Graham murmured her name, his chest flush against her back as he continued to drive her mad. She leaned forward, licking Colin's shoulder. His muscles tensed beneath her lips, and he groaned more loudly. Graham cursed again, dragging his teeth over her shoulder as he seemed to grow inside her. As for her? She was slowly going out of her mind.

She knew she wouldn't last much longer. Her every sense was filled with them. Their touch. Their smell. Their taste. Everything crashed over her in the next moment, sending her spiraling toward an orgasm so intense she stopped breathing and just arched wildly between them. She rode the crest, peaking higher still as they were wild inside her now.

"I'm coming!" Colin shouted. "Ah, God, I can't hold it any longer."

"Let go," Graham bit out. "I'm with you."

She heard all of this as if from far away, her mind spinning as she closed her eyes and trusted them to keep her grounded when she finally came back down. They shuddered and quaked around her, inside of her, and she began to sob. It was all just too much.

"I love you!" she sobbed, burying her head in the crook of Colin's neck. "Oh, I love you both."

Graham withdrew and fell against her, stroking her back and kissing her cheek. "Ah, Lily," he said, breathing in deeply. He ran his lips over her shoulder and gently nibbled on her flesh. "I love you, too."

She froze, her heart skidding to a stop. She had to be hearing things. Her climax must have rattled something loose in her head. Graham loved her?

Shaking her head, she slowly turned to catch his beautiful Hawk eyes staring into hers. They were solemn and intense and held an emotion she'd never seen before. "Graham?"

"I love you, Lily," he said again, his voice steady despite the rapid heartbeat she felt against her.

"W–what?" she stammered.

"He loves you," Colin said, collapsing beneath her and bringing her down to the bed with him. He withdrew as well and held her stretched out over him. "I love you, too."

She shifted, turning to better face Colin. "What did you say?"

Graham caught her chin and tilted her to face him. "We both love you, Lily. We want a future with you."

Oh no. It was as she feared. Scrambling a bit, she slid off of Colin and sat on the bed. She pulled her knees to her chest and buried her face in her hands. "I have no future."

Tears choked her as she came to one horrid conclusion. They wanted her in their bed. She tugged at the sheets and brought them up over her breasts and nodded as she realized the truth. She loved them so much she couldn't imagine being their mistress. Yet she wanted to be with them forever. "All right." She lifted her head and swiped at her tears. "I'll come with you."

Colin blinked, his blue eyes clouded. "I certainly hope so."

Graham took her shaking hands in his. "Lily, what's wrong?"

"I love you both, Graham. Both of you. I cannot stay here at the manor. Not once Lady Hawksfell learns of what I did!"

Graham smiled, cupping her face so gently she nearly cried from the tenderness. "Lady Hawksfell won't care one whit when she learns you're to be my wife."

The bed seemed to dip beneath her and she clutched on to her knees. "What are you saying?"

Colin clicked his tongue. "Not the right words, apparently." He took one of her hands in his. "Graham is asking you to marry him, Lily."

She gazed into his beautiful blue eyes and began to cry again.

* * * *

Graham stared at Lily's stricken face, completely at a loss. "Lily, what's wrong?"

"Oh, how can I marry you? I'm nothing!"

His heart flipped, and he looked to Colin for help. He also looked confused as he helplessly shook his head.

"Lily," Graham began, determined to clarify matters. "You are not nothing. You're everything."

She shook her head. "I'm just a maid, Graham. A maid who had nothing but the good opinion of her employer and now I won't even have that."

"The countess cares very much for you," Colin said. "Don't you know that?"

"Now, perhaps. But what about when she learns of this." She waved a hand to indicate their three naked bodies still so close on the bed. "And Mrs. Holmes, who had always been so kind to me. She's been like a m–mother!"

"You know, she all but raised the earl," Graham said. "Surely she knows of the Hawk curse."

When she paled, he knew that had been the wrong thing to say.

"This was all because of the curse?" she screeched. Tears poured down her dear face as she twisted the sheets in her hands. "I'd heard of a dark history at the manor before I came here." She sniffled, dragging a hand over her cheeks and blinking her remarkable green eyes. "A strong lust that ran in the Hawk men. Something about the servants and every Hawk in history. Cabot had said something..."

Graham thought of that afternoon he'd found Cabot teasing her out by the garage. "Tell me you didn't take the word of that boy who just wanted to get under your skirts," he said.

She stared at him for a beat. "And what happened after you discouraged Cabot, Graham? Didn't you manage to get under my skirts?"

"Now, Lily," Colin started but Lily gave a firm shake of her head.

"Why didn't I press the other servants for more information?" she asked.

"Maybe their loyalty to the earl kept them quiet?" Colin offered.

Graham nodded. "That's a very good thing, I wager. It would have been a tragedy if you had known about it from the first."

Her eyes widened and she sniffled again. "What are you saying? My ignorance made this..." She waved a hand over the bed again. "This liaison easy for your both?"

"No, Lily," Graham said.

"Was keeping me in the dark just what you had planned all along?" she asked, her voice taking on that screeching quality again. "To take advantage of me?"

Graham swore to himself and tried to take a different tack. "God, I'm making a royal mess of this."

Colin chuckled. "Yes, you are. Lily, Graham loves you. His curse is something Hawks either surrender to or break. Do you know how they manage to break that curse and live a happy life?"

She shook her head but he saw the acute interest on her face.

"Love," Colin said. "With all these happy Hawks in and around the manor? Surely you saw evidence of that happiness."

"I love you," Graham said. "Colin loves you. Can't you see what the three of us can be?"

She blinked those incredible eyes and stared at him. "The *three* of us?"

"Could you bear to be without either one of us?" he asked.

"No," she said without hesitation.

He found himself smiling. "And I can't imagine a life without you and Colin in it."

"You love Colin?" she asked.

"I do. And he loves me."

"You both love me?"

They nodded and the light in her beautiful eyes was stunning to see.

"We do," Colin said.

Her gaze slid away as she fingered the sheets now down around her slender waist. "I never thought I would find passion, not after what the old baron did to me."

Graham exchanged a look with Colin, but they both knew she had to talk about that horrific time at her previous position.

"I never thought I would *want* to experience everything you two have shown me." She raised her head and stared at the two of them. "I want you both, Colin. I love you both, Graham. My body and my heart…" She shrugged. "You two are everything I could want."

"You love us," Graham stated. He wasn't going to take anything less than that admission, now that their bodies had cooled. "You love us both."

Colin smiled and tucked a strand of hair behind her ear. "So will you spend the rest of your life with us, Lily?"

She bit her lip and nodded, her eyes bright. "I will gladly spend the rest of my life with the only two men I have ever loved."

"Then I guess Lady Hawksfell will have to find another new maid," Graham said.

Lily's lovely, expressive face showed her every emotion, and Graham didn't need her to say the words again. She loved him. Loved him and Colin both.

He held her close as the three of them settled down on the bed. He marveled at what had happened to him since coming to Hawksfell Manor. He'd found a family in Gabriel and the other Hawks. A sense of belonging he never had with his great aunt and uncle despite their kindness. More than that, he'd found a love he'd never expected and finally recognized one he'd always had.

This might have all started as a game. By giving up the pretense he usually wore, he became the man he never thought he could be. A man worthy of Colin's love. Worthy of Lily's love. Worthy of a future he never realized he wanted.

Life might indeed be a game, but he wouldn't play it by his own rules any longer. No. He'd live his life with Lily and Colin.

This was a game they'd all win.

THE END

WWW.JOSIEDENNIS.COM

Siren Publishing

Ménage Amour

Josie Dennis

Lords of Hawksfell Manor 6

Victor's Vow

VICTOR'S VOW

Lords of Hawksfell Manor 6

JOSIE DENNIS
Copyright © 2014

Chapter 1

Yorkshire, England 1912

Victor Hawk, Baron Ralston, stared up at the canopy over his very large, very lonely bed. His cock was hard, like it was nearly every night of his life since reaching manhood.

"Not tonight, damn it," he groaned into the dark.

He wouldn't seek release. No, this was his penance for being born a Hawk. He was twenty-seven years old and this had been his lot for nearly half that time.

He rolled onto his side, wincing as the fine sheets brushed over him. His heart thudded in beat to his throbbing shaft, and he squeezed his eyes shut. Images from tonight's dinner crashed through his mind as he relived the torture of sitting across from Violet as she delicately picked at her meal. Her blonde hair had caught the lights and her flawless skin had flushed rosy from the fire burning in the hearth. She was an innocent. He knew that. She was his late mother's niece of sorts, and his third cousin. It was to her credit that she'd come to help care for his mother over the past year. She'd proven invaluable, and he was squarely in her debt. He wouldn't repay that debt by rutting on her like a damned Hawk.

They hadn't spoken much during dinner, which was not unusual for them, and he'd escaped her company right after. The house was like a tomb, and had been for the three months since his mother died. And for nearly a year prior as well, if he were being completely honest. He dated that condition from when his mother fell ill and Violet moved in to help with her care.

Ah, Violet. She was a complication he didn't need. It was difficult enough, denying his cursed Hawk lusts all day and all night. With merely a whiff of her floral scent, as light as the flower she was named for, he went from semi-hard to aching for release in an instant. Now that they lived beneath the same roof essentially alone, there was truly nothing to stop him from indulging every fantasy he'd ever had about her. Of lifting the skirts of her somber gowns to reveal what he suspected was a gorgeous pussy and tasting her. Of holding on to her round little bottom and fucking her hard from behind. God, she was sweet and fresh and everything he didn't deserve.

He wrapped his hands around his shaft, knowing he couldn't find release that way. He'd tried several times, only to earn debilitating pain in his belly and an excruciating erection that lasted for hours. Dragging his thumb over the tip, he hissed as he felt a drop of cream. He had to come. He'd never sleep if he didn't find relief.

Easing himself out of bed, he went to the pull and rang for one of the maids. He didn't care which one. He needed to come and he needed to come now. Donning his dressing gown, he sat beside the crackling hearth and tried to relax even as his body was humming. When a soft knock came at the door, he nearly growled in anticipation.

"Come," he called.

The door was opened and a maid entered. The girl was one he'd never seen before. That was good, for he couldn't bring himself to use someone more than once. He saw that they were amply rewarded and treated well, but he let his man-of-affairs handle the particulars. The man must have hired some new staff, not that Victor usually gave any care to the running of Ralston House.

His estate was successful, due to his Hawk heritage. Hawks were blessed with handling money. That was true. That blessing wasn't much consolation given his raging lust and his weakness to resist it. Tonight's surrender was a prime example.

"Do you need me, my lord?" the maid asked.

He spread his robe and let his cock free. She came to stand in front of him. He closed his eyes and swallowed down his cold shame as she dropped to her knees on the fine carpet.

Afterward, when the girl left, he climbed back into his bed. He'd come deep down her throat, his orgasm almost painful as he'd bucked and groaned his release. In that scalding hot moment of release he'd pictured Violet before him, her rosebud lips wrapped around his cock as she stroked him up and down until he exploded.

Shutting his eyes, he tried to set it all from his mind. Sadness that his mother was gone. Guilt that he hadn't been able to fight his Hawk lusts yet again.

And shame that he wanted to take his innocent cousin.

* * * *

Violet Ralston sat in the breakfast room, ready for another long and lonely day. Victor wasn't about, and she guessed he'd ridden out on the estate early despite the bitter December day's chill.

He had been his usual dour self at dinner last night, but only when his dark Hawk eyes hadn't run over her. He'd obviously thought she hadn't been aware of his close regard throughout their meal, but how could she not be? From the moment she'd come to Ralston House last year he'd been the only one in her thoughts. The spicy, hot scent of him. The scalding heat of his big body. The dark rumors of his sensual Hawk curse. It all still sent her virginal body into spasms of heated fantasies she doubted she would ever see fulfilled.

She knew he made use of their servants. His mother, her dear

Aunt Jane, had divulged as much during a particularly dark day last spring. The woman blamed herself for Victor's condition, saying that if she hadn't succumbed to a Hawk she wouldn't have indulged and bore a child. True, Victor's father had returned once he was born to legitimatize him but he'd never spent any time with her aunt or Victor that Violet knew of.

Victor certainly never spoke of his father, or any other Hawk relatives for that matter. Her aunt never said much about Victor's father or about the Hawks in general, other than their high lusts and shameful desires. As for Violet, more than once she longed to ask one of the maids just what Victor did to satisfy his particular beast.

Did he take them hard, his big body driving into their softness to find release? Did they put their hands on his...cock until he reached his pinnacle? Oh, if only she knew something about passion she could envision matters more clearly. For a woman of twenty-three years, she was woefully ignorant.

"Miss Ralston?" the butler said from the doorway.

She faced the elderly gentleman. "Yes, Wilson?"

"A letter has arrived for Lord Ralston."

Violet blinked. "And?"

"He is out, miss."

"I reasoned that, Wilson. Why don't you leave it in the salver?"

The butler shook his head. "I think not, miss. This is from the Earl of Hawksfell."

Violet's mouth dropped open. Even *she* had heard of the earl, the head of the Hawk family here in Yorkshire. He was purported to be the most virile and demanding of all the Hawks but to her knowledge Victor had never made his acquaintance.

"Why would the earl write to Vic...to Lord Ralston?" she asked.

The butler's cheeks reddened. "It isn't my place to answer."

She held out her hand. "I'll give it to the baron, Wilson."

Wilson looked as though a heavy weight had been lifted as he handed over the letter. She placed it beside her plate on the table, eyeing it as she finished drinking her tea. Well, at least she would have an excuse to speak to Victor today. She admitted to herself that it was a comfort to know he would have to pay attention to her, if only on this matter.

It was a pity he would never pay her the particular attention she craved.

* * * *

When Victor came in from his ride she was ready for him. She'd been waiting in the parlor for the past half hour for him to make an appearance. The fire crackled behind the grate, warm and merry, but her hands felt cold. The letter from Lord Hawksfell sat on the table beside her chair, and her head ached from trying to figure out just what possibility it could present. She'd finally just put that darn thing on the table to await Victor's compelling eyes.

He stalked into the parlor through the glass doors at the back of the house, and her breath caught. The wind had made his cheeks ruddy and he exuded masculine strength. His thick dark hair was dusted with a few snowflakes which sparkled as they rapidly melted. Her pulse leapt and she stifled a sigh.

"Hello, Victor," she managed to say.

He froze, his dark eyes snapping toward her. "Violet?" He pulled off his gloves with deliberate tugs. "What are you doing here?"

"Here at Ralston House?"

He waved a hand. "No. Here in the parlor."

"Did you think to avoid me?" She'd tried for a light, teasing tone but flirtation was never her forte. "That is, where did you think I would be?"

"I don't know." He shrugged and took off his long coat, placing it over the back of the chair across from her. "The library?"

It was a valid answer. She spent quite a bit of time lost in those books now that she no longer had to care for her aunt.

"Nevertheless, here I sit." She picked up the letter from the earl. "This came for you."

He blinked and took a step toward her. Oh, she could smell him now. She held the letter out to him.

"Why do you have it?" he asked, taking the letter and turning it over.

"Wilson didn't want to leave it in the salver," she answered with a shrug.

"The Earl of Hawksfell," he read aloud. He studied the letter and she could tell he was intrigued. His nostrils flared and his fingers traced over the seal. "What could he possibly want?"

"There is one way to find out," she said.

He lifted his head, pinning her with those eyes. Then he flashed her a curve of his lips that might be considered a smile. "Right."

He broke the seal and unfolded the paper within. As she watched, a flicker of emotion crossed his rugged features, accompanied by a narrowing of his eyes as he read the earl's words. His sculpted lips parted for a moment, then pressed into a thin line. "Preposterous."

She was fairly trembling with curiosity as she considered just what the earl had to say. "What is it, Victor?"

"He wants me to come to Hawksfell Manor." He dropped the hand holding the letter to his side. "To meet the other Hawk relatives."

It was her turn to let her mouth gape open. "The other Hawks?"

"Yes, the earl and his brother. As well as a few cousins."

She heard something in his voice, a wistfulness she'd never heard before. "Never say you're going."

His brows drew together. "I don't suppose I should feel compelled, but…"

Realization struck her then. He *wanted* to meet the other Hawks, despite the lack of any indication he'd ever given in the past. Rising out of her chair, she reached out to touch his arm. "You should go."

He looked down at her hand, then into her eyes. The floor tilted beneath her and she forced herself to remain still.

"You deserve to have someone else in your life," she said softly.

"Other than you, you mean?" he asked, his voice rough.

Her throat tightened. "Victor…"

He dropped the letter and grabbed her upper arms. "Violet, are you tired of me?"

She blinked rapidly. Her emotions were a riot inside of her. "What? I don't understand."

He brought his face close to hers. "You came here for my mother. You can leave Ralston House at any time."

Swallowing thickly, she tried to think of a reasonable answer. There was really only one, however. "You know as well as I that I have nowhere else to go."

He nodded and brought his mouth to hers, his lips brushing over her flesh. She could scarcely breathe. He kissed her, at first quite softly then with a hard press of his mouth before he set her from him.

"Victor?" she managed to ask.

"Nowhere else to go," he repeated, reaching down to pick up the discarded letter. His eyes were intent on her before he turned away. "That is a pity."

With long strides, he left the parlor. Sinking back into the chair, she touched her fingertips to her mouth. His taste was like his scent, spicy and hot. She closed her eyes and reveled in the memory of that too-brief kiss.

It was a lamentable truth she couldn't ignore. That would most likely be the only kiss she ever got from him.

Chapter 2

"You look quite pretty standing there, Cabot."

Cabot Reilly looked over at the new lady's maid poised against the wall opposite. With auburn hair and deep brown eyes, Ivy was a pretty thing, though she had nothing on her predecessor. No, Lily was a remarkable beauty.

"Lady Hawksfell isn't in need of your services, Ivy?" he asked, giving her a smile.

Her eyes widened, then her lips tilted in a grin. "Not at present."

He was adept at flirting. He knew that. More than one girl had fallen into his bed in the past two years since he'd come to Hawksfell Manor. Yet his charm hadn't gained him anything but frustration with the last maid he'd fancied. No, Lily was now wed to yet another Hawk man.

It seemed that the Hawks who came to visit the Earl of Hawksfell found true love or something or other. He didn't really hold much to the theory of love, despite the earl's apparently happy marriage. His parents had certainly never been happy on the farm. Oh, they'd seemed content but he'd never seen any passion there. More than once he wondered if he'd been left at the farm by fairies. Yes, he had his mother's blonde hair and blue eyes but in mood and temperament he'd always felt out of place.

Here at the manor, though? Here he felt in his element. He was poised to take over the position of first footman, once William vacated it sometime in the near future. William was also involved with a Hawk man, along with the pretty little former parlor maid Posy. Yet another woman put out of his own reach, not that he'd really had chance with either Posy or Lily. No, both those girls had seemed immune to his particular brand of charm. This one, however, seemed ready for a tumble.

"I'm waiting for Mr. Carstairs' orders, Ivy," he said, letting his eyes run over her, taking in her crisp uniform and pristine apron. The little lace cap on top of her head was straight and her hair was neat and tidy. "Not all of us have such an undemanding employer."

Ivy shrugged, an obvious gesture that drew her blouse tight against her ample breasts. "It's true Lady Hawksfell doesn't like to be fussed over." Her eyes ran over the front of his trousers and his body began to react. "I'm content to watch you standing at attention, as it were."

He waited for the rush of heat the exchange should bring. For his heart to pound as his blood rushed to his cock. It wouldn't take much to make himself respond to her. She was lovely and built for pleasure. That was certain. Did he want to start up something with another servant, though? For the first time in his memory he didn't believe so.

He glanced down the hallway and saw that no one was about. He was in the bachelor's wing, seeing that the rooms were ready for another Hawk to visit within the next few days. These rooms were far from the family bedrooms though, which confirmed his supposition that Ivy was ready for a ride. Not only did she have no business in this part of the house but they were far from any other servants at this time of day. Stepping away from the wall at his back, he came to stand very close to her.

She swayed toward him and placed a hand on his arm. "These rooms are vacant, Cabot." She licked her full lips. "The manor has no visitors at present."

He let his body brush against hers. "Never say you want a tumble, Ivy."

"With you?" Her eyes flared. "Oh, I've heard you give a woman a good ride."

That comment stilled him. She'd heard about him, then. From whom? He'd pleased a good many of the maids and a few of the grooms over the past two years. Though after the business with the earl's particular rules of employment, he didn't believe anyone would speak of such matters. Not now that the earl was happily married and no longer needed release from his staff.

"You've heard?" He braced his hands on either side of her head and leaned close. "From whom?"

She shrugged, her cheeks going pink. "Not *heard*, precisely. No one would tell me anything about what goes on at the manor."

"What went on," he corrected automatically.

He immediately regretted his words. Interest showed in her big brown eyes.

"What went on, Cabot?" she asked, breathless.

He thought for a way out. God, maybe he should just fuck her to shut her up. He felt loyalty to the earl for giving him this position with no experience. He knew he'd been hired because he was tall and considered handsome, as a good footman in a great house should be. If he'd had to please the earl before that business ended, he didn't want anyone speaking of it. Certainly not this pert maid so newly come to Hawksfell.

"Go below to see if Mrs. Holmes needs your help, then," he said. He softened the dismissal with another smile. "You'll find Mrs. Holmes a caring housekeeper and a gentle woman." *And a person who doesn't pass or allow gossip in the servants hall.*

Ivy nodded even as she blinked in confusion. "She is kind."

He just stepped away, straightening his jacket. "I'll see you after dinner service, Ivy."

She nodded, her eyes downcast now. "Indeed." With that she left for the stairs down to the servants hall.

He breathed a sigh of relief as he headed in the opposite direction. He could have taken her into one of the guest rooms along this corridor and fucked her until she couldn't walk straight. It would have shut her inquisitive mouth and eased his own frustrations. As he passed through the family wing and went down the main stairs to the ground floor, he thought about the past months since the earl's marriage.

More than one damn Hawk had come to the manor, some with their lovers in tow, some with their minds set on stealing one or another member of the earl's loyal staff. Even as he thought that he knew he wasn't being fair in the assessment, however. Over the past months quite a few marriages had taken place with a Hawk man at the center. One or the other of that Hawk's lovers did prove to be a maid or footman, though. It was passing strange. He'd never imagined servants could mingle with people of quality. Yet all he'd seen suggested they'd found love here.

"Love," he muttered as he reached the servants hall.

"What's that, Cabot?" Mr. Carstairs asked.

The stout butler was imposing and still frightened Cabot a little bit. "Nothing, Mr. Carstairs."

"I take it the rooms in the bachelor wing are readied?"

"Yes, Mr. Carstairs. How is this Hawk related to the earl?"

Most of the Hawks were cousins but there was the time the earl's previously unknown half brother came to stay. He was now Posy's husband, actually.

The butler bristled, his round face going a little red. "It is not our place to inquire, Cabot."

Cabot kept his expression even and the butler eased in his rigidity.

"It seems another Hawk cousin is indeed coming for a visit, however," Mr. Carstairs finished.

For some reason, the confirmation made Cabot feel out of sorts.

"The rooms are ready, Mr. Carstairs," he said.

The butler nodded. "Good, good. I don't know if he will arrive alone, however." His lips thinned. "I believe I'll have one of the maids see to the rooms near the family wing as well."

Cabot's brows rose. A woman was coming as well? He knew he couldn't ask that question of Mr. Carstairs. The man would turn apoplectic at such open curiosity. Instead, he just nodded and went to see about dinner service. His mind was churning, though. *Was* this newest Hawk coming alone? The last one came with his friend in tow, and both men had swept Lily off her delicate feet. Fucked her, too. Hard and often before making an honest woman of her.

He didn't fault Lily one bit for succumbing to Graham Hawk's raw sexuality. He himself had been attracted to all of the Hawks who visited. He was able to admit that to himself. They were all of them much like the earl himself. Big and strong with those compellingly dark Hawk eyes. No doubt all would fall under this new Hawk's spell upon his arrival, whether he brought a gentleman or a lady with him or arrived alone.

Cabot went to the long table in the common room and settled into a chair. What was it to him if they got up to something?

"Let them fuck Ivy," he grumbled.

He would just focus on his work and put all thoughts of sex and Hawks out of his mind.

* * * *

Victor sat before the fire the next afternoon, mulling over the response he'd sent to the Earl of Hawksfell. He'd decided to accept the man's offer and, in a flash of foolishness, added that he wouldn't be arriving alone. He was going to ask Violet to accompany him. His gut told him it was a big mistake to take her along, yet his heart ached when he thought of her alone in this big house. The memory of the hurt in those gorgeous violet eyes of hers still cut him. "No place else to go," she'd said. As much as he longed to get away from the temptation she posed every day, he couldn't leave her here.

He hadn't broached the subject yet, however. He suspected that, deep down, his motives were less pure on that count. Perhaps if he got her away from Ralston House he could find a way to indulge in a few fantasies without ruining her. Maybe kissing her some more or touching her pussy to make her come. His Hawk beast swiftly rose and he cursed.

"Not again," he muttered.

"What is that, Victor?" Violet asked.

He breathed in, letting her scent waft over him from the doorway. "Nothing, Violet."

She tilted her blonde head, a gesture of innocence that nonetheless had a pull for him of which he was certain she was unaware.

"Are you off for Hawksfell, then?" she asked.

He heard a note of sadness in her voice and straightened. "Sit, Violet," he said, waving to the chair opposite.

Her long lashes fluttered but she did as he bade. She folded her hands in her lap. "What is it?"

He took in a breath and stared into her eyes for a heartbeat. "I want you to come to Hawksfell Manor with me."

Her lovely mouth gaped open. "You want..." More lash fluttering followed and a stain of pink spread over her cheeks. "You want me to come with you?"

"I'm not comfortable leaving you here alone." It was all he would admit to. "This house is too damned quiet."

She bit her lip for a moment and then her eyes lit with obvious delight at the prospect. "Oh, I hear the manor is most impressive!" She clasped her hands. "Are you certain they won't mind an unexpected guest? I wouldn't want to intrude on your family visit."

He shook his head. "I've already let them know that you're coming with me. Besides, it's hardly a family visit."

She eyed him, then nodded. "They are your family, Victor."

He sneered. "Hawks."

To his shock she rose and joined him on the chair. She was a small thing, but there was still hardly room for her to squeeze in next to his big body. Her ass slid over his hip as she settled beside him and took one of his hands in hers. Her fingers felt fragile clasped to his large ones.

"They are your family, Victor. Perhaps this visit will do you some good."

He studied her face then let his gaze dip down to her décolletage. Her bosom was plump and rosy and he could glimpse the enticing shadow between her breasts. His beast stirred again and he squeezed her hand.

"*Some* good, Violet?" he asked, bringing his face to hers. "Do you believe I at least deserve that?"

Her eyes were deep dark purple now. Her tongue flicked out to wet her luscious lips and he leaned closer still.

"Victor…"

He kissed her again. It was like yesterday but so much more. Plunging his tongue into her sweet mouth, he took what he wanted. She whimpered, then moaned softly. There was no mistaking the pleasure in that sound. It was all the invitation he needed.

"God, Violet." He dragged his lips over her smooth cheek and down to her throat.

A stroke of his tongue at the base revealed the flutter of her pulse. She turned in the chair, and her breasts rubbed against his chest as she reached up to grab onto his shoulders. He'd never touched her before, aside from that first brief kiss, but his fingers itched to stroke her. His urgency was great enough to make up for any fumbling at the back of her dress. He'd never had to undress a woman whose corset laced in the back. Hell, he'd never undressed any of the maids he'd fucked either.

He managed to loosen her corset enough to ease it away from her breasts and before she could do more than gasp he tugged down her chemise and had her bared to his eyes.

She was beautiful. Her breasts were round and white and topped with rosy pink nipples. His mouth watered. He bent his head and breathed in her scent. Then he closed his mouth over one bud and sucked hard.

"Oh, my!" she cried, clutching at his head.

He licked and teethed her as his hand found its way up under her skirt. She froze for an instant, then parted her smooth thighs just enough to let him sneak two fingers very near her pussy. Her drawers were damp and he could feel her heat.

"You're wet," he marveled aloud. "God, you're wet and hot."

He was seized with a wildness as he stroked her as deep and hard as he dared. Her little moans of delight told him she was close, and when he pinched her clit she cried out. Placing his mouth on hers, he kissed her as he drove her over the edge. Her juices soaked his fingers as she trembled in his arms.

He eased away from her and slowly withdrew his hand from under her skirt. He was shaking now, his cock about to burst if he didn't find release soon. She, on the other hand, was languid against the arm of the chair, a look of bliss on her face.

"Oh, Victor." Her eyes opened and she gazed at him. "What you did to me…"

Her breasts were still bare and bore faint red marks from the bristles on his jaw. He longed for another taste. "I hadn't meant to."

She must have heard the pain in his voice despite his effort to restrain it. Her brow furrowed over worried eyes.

Pulling up the bodice of her dress, she leaned toward him. "What's wrong?" Her hand inadvertently touched his shaft and he winced. She dropped her gaze to his trousers, her eyes going wide. "Your cock."

His mouth dropped open. "How do you know about such things?"

She shrugged, her eyes never leaving his crotch. "I'd heard about you, Victor." She met his gaze then. "About your needs."

He wasn't going to discuss his dark needs with this innocent girl. As he started to rise, she placed her hand on his cock and he realized she might not be as innocent as he thought. "Violet!"

His buttons gave way easily and she reached inside to grasp him. He hissed at the sensation of her fingers on his skin.

"Let me ease you, Victor," she said, her face serious. "Oh, you are as large as they say."

"H–how do you know…?" He closed his eyes and swallowed a groan as she stroked him. "How the hell do you know how to ease me?"

She laughed softly and he opened his eyes. She was blushing as she awkwardly, and very effectively, rubbed the head of his cock. "Don't you know one of the best features of living in a large house, Victor?"

He swallowed again and shook his head.

She stroked him long and slow. "The gossip."

He wrapped his hand around hers, giving up any resistance to letting her release him. He needed to come and he couldn't do it alone.

"Let me show you the particulars," he bit out.

She stared down at him and licked her lips and he did groan at last. He was going to explode any moment now. Again and again their hands moved over his shaft, her soft fingers between his own hand and his flesh. Just a few more strokes and then he came with a shout, trembling against her as he spilled his seed on his trousers.

"Oh, my," she said as she had earlier.

He blew out a breath and removed her hand from him. Tucking his cock back in his pants, he withdrew a handkerchief and wiped up as best he could. Sliding his gaze to hers, he waited for the revulsion to strike her. To his surprise she smiled.

"You're better now," she said.

He stood. "Yes, I've recovered."

"Recovered?" She blinked up at him. "It's not a malady, Victor."

"Isn't it?" He ran his fingers through his hair and turned away. "I can't control myself, Violet. Apparently my damned Hawk lusts are so high I let my dear cousin give me pleasure."

"Dear?" Her voice held a hope he couldn't let her foster.

"You'd be wise to stay away from me," he said. "For my part, I promise to never touch you again."

Her skirts rustled as she came to her feet. "Never?"

He couldn't look at her. She'd have that expression of adoration she'd worn after he gave her what he knew for certain was her first orgasm. She was already dependent on him. He wouldn't have her fancying herself in love with him, too.

"Go, Violet. Ready your things for tomorrow."

"Then you still wish for me to come with you to Hawksfell Manor?"

Her voice was tremulous and he cursed himself. He couldn't cause her even more pain tonight. He faced her at last. Her clothes were rumpled, her hair mussed and her eyes huge in her flushed and lovely face.

"I said you'd be accompanying me, didn't I?" he asked her a little too sharply.

She gave a shaky nod and hurried from the room.

"Damn it." He sank down into the chair once more. The scent of their sex mingled and he couldn't help but breathe in deeply.

And now he was going to meet his Hawk relatives with her in tow. He cursed.

"What the hell have I done?"

Chapter 3

"Another Hawk is to arrive," Ivy said, her voice trembling with obvious excitement.

Cabot kept his features even as he stepped away from her to find his place in line with the other servants assembled on the drive. The day was bitter cold but they were all to meet the arriving guests as was expected. At least the wind wasn't blowing on this side of the house and the sun was bright.

Mr. Carstairs and Mrs. Holmes were at the front of the line, followed by Grayson, Lord Hawksfell's valet. Ivy stood beside him as Lady Hawksfell's maid. Cabot was a bit farther down the line as footman but he still had an unobstructed view of the fine motor making its way toward the manor.

As it rolled smoothly to a stop on the drive, he felt a flicker of excitement. Yes, this was another Hawk. Yes, this was another man no doubt gifted and cursed as all the Hawks were. He would be lying if he said he wasn't interested in this one, though.

The chauffeur jumped out of the car and opened the back door. A slight figure stepped out, wrapped in a fine cloak. Cabot could glimpse a shapely figure beneath, however. He had a talent for spotting a pair of fine breasts despite any cover. The woman lifted her head and her hood fell back, revealing hair as blonde as his own. Her face was exquisite, an oval dominated by large dark blue eyes. He stared at her exposed throat, seeing the smooth taut skin. For an instant he wondered if he placed his face in the hollow of her throat would she smell as sweet as she looked.

He'd never really looked at the ladies who came to the manor, since they were so far above him. Why risk refusal when he could just fuck a maid? This girl was astounding, though. Her full lips parted as she gazed up at the manor, all the way toward the attic rooms that were the servants quarters. She was obviously impressed, but then who wouldn't be?

Built of soaring sandstone walls topped by peaked slate roofs and too many windows to count, Hawksfell Manor was indeed a grand home. Once again he felt proud and honored to work there.

"Hello," she said in a husky, lovely voice.

Mr. Carstairs stepped forward.

"Welcome to Hawksfell Manor, Miss..."

"Miss Ralston," the man stepping out of the motor offered. "My third cousin."

Cabot glanced at him and his breath caught. God, he was as beautiful as the earl himself. Same glossy black hair and tall, strong build. But it was those dark Hawk eyes that sent a lick of lust over his body.

"Baron Ralston," the butler said with a bow of his head. "Welcome to Hawksfell Manor. I am Carstairs, the butler, and this is the housekeeper, Mrs. Holmes."

"Thank you, Carstairs." The baron turned his head to regard the housekeeper. "Mrs. Holmes."

The housekeeper's eyes narrowed for an instant and Cabot could guess her thoughts. No doubt she wondered if this Hawk would get up to the exploits the others had without exception. In a flash he imagined the two visitors, the baron dark and his cousin fair, locked in an embrace. The image of the baron's big body pounding into her delicate one made him grateful it was so cold outside this afternoon. Even with the chill his cock twitched to attention.

"Did you bring your man, my lord?" Mr. Carstairs asked.

The baron shook his head. "I'm afraid he stays back at Ralston House."

"Then allow me to offer you Cabot's services during your stay."

Cabot swallowed. Yes, he'd served several visiting Hawk men over the past few months but he'd never been so attracted to any of them. "It would be my honor," he managed to say, dipping his head.

Lord Ralston caught his eye at last and Cabot was struck by something other than lust. This particular Hawk looked somber. Almost sad. A quick look at his companion showed an answering melancholy in her big violet eyes. There was something about these two newcomers, but he was damned if he knew what it was precisely. They were beautiful. There was no question. And connected, if the lady's close proximity to the baron was any indication.

They passed him and he hurried to see to Lord Ralston's portmanteaux. The deep timbre of his voice mingling with Miss Ralston's delicate husky one caused a riot of disturbance within him. He'd never been a randy bunch of hormones, despite his many conquests and his apparent reputation. Yet, this afternoon…

"Put the baron in the blue room, Cabot," Mrs. Holmes said. "We'll see Miss Ralston's things settled closer to the family."

He nodded. Thankful to have something to occupy himself, he made his way up the stairs toward the bachelor wing. He wouldn't think about dressing and undressing the very impressive baron this evening. He wouldn't think about serving at the table and watching the gorgeous Miss Ralston as she ate, either. He had no idea how long they would stay at Hawksfell Manor. His cock was half-hard and he wasn't even near either one of them at present.

"Maybe I should just fuck Ivy," he muttered to himself.

The pretty maid didn't cause the intense attraction within him that the manor's two newest visitors did, however.

And he knew in his heart there was nothing he could do about it.

* * * *

"I've sent Ivy up to see to Miss Ralston, my lord," the housekeeper told Victor. "Lady Hawksfell insisted on lending her maid's services during her visit."

Victor nodded to the woman. She looked capable and almost kind and not what he was expecting. She had a motherly quality and the loss of his own mother bit at him.

"Thank you, Mrs. Holmes. I'm sure Violet... Miss Ralston will be comfortable."

A slight flick of the housekeeper's eyebrows told him she'd caught his verbal slip. Wonderful.

"I believe the earl is awaiting you in his study," she said. "Cabot, do show him the way."

Victor turned and saw the handsome young footman he'd spied when he'd first arrived. He was tall and leanly muscled, but his coloring brought Violet to mind. The two could be twins, if Cabot's eyes were a shade darker.

"Yes, Mrs. Holmes," the footman said.

There was a touch of resignation in his voice. Was the footman put upon to see to the earl's visitor? He'd seemed to welcome the added duty as his valet out on the drive. Victor shook his head and followed the man toward the back of the manor.

As they walked down the corridor, Victor couldn't help but admire the earl's home. It was quite grand and impressive and decorated much like Ralston House. It was far larger, however. The earl was blessed with money as all Hawks were, then. Was he cursed with the dark lusts as well?

"Baron Ralston, my lord," the footman announced.

Cabot turned and met his gaze for a moment and Victor felt a rush of heat travel up his cheeks. The footman passed him and he shook his head again. He must still be befuddled from his ride here with Violet. He couldn't be attracted to a man he'd seen for only a moment.

He stepped into the room and faced a tall, imposing gentleman standing behind a large carved wood desk.

"Welcome to Hawksfell," the earl said with a smile.

Victor stared at this Hawk man he'd never met. It was much like looking in a mirror. The same cleft chin and chiseled cheeks, dark hair and eyes as well. "Hello, Lord Hawksfell."

"Please, call me Gabriel."

Victor inclined his head. "Gabriel. Call me Victor, then."

"Sit, Victor." The earl settled behind the desk and Victor sat in the chair opposite. "I'm glad you accepted my invitation. You and your, third cousin is it?"

Victor nodded. "Forgive me for the presumptuousness, but I couldn't in good conscience leave her at home alone."

"Nothing to forgive. I know how close family can be."

There was something in the earl's tone that niggled at the back of his mind. He was married, that much he'd gleaned from the letter. But what was this about family?

"No, you misunderstand," Victor began. "Violet, Miss Ralston, had been caring for my mother."

"And she's recently passed," Gabriel said. "I'm sorry for your loss."

"Thank you. The house is just so…"

"Sad?"

"It is depressing," Victor admitted. "I didn't want her there alone."

"As you've said." Gabriel's dark eyes danced for a moment before his expression sobered. "You and Miss Ralston are welcome here as long as you wish to stay."

"Again, thank you for the invitation. But I must know why you sent for me."

The earl leaned back in his chair. "It seems I've taken on the habit of seeking out wayward Hawks, Victor." He smiled. It was a very nice smile and Victor found himself returning the expression. "You are the most recent to come to the roost, as it were."

"The Hawk's roost," Victor said. "Yet, you're recently married."

"Indeed. I wed this past summer." He glanced out the window at the snow-covered landscape beyond. "God, has it been five months already? Well, my brother and a few Hawk cousins have stepped into the parson's trap over the past months so forgive me if I lost track of the passage of time."

The earl barked out a laugh and Victor couldn't help but chuckle. "Well, don't expect to attend a wedding on my account."

Gabriel arched a brow. "No? Ah, well. It's still good to have family about."

"You mentioned a brother. Does he live nearby?"

"Matthew is my half brother, actually. And yes, he lives in the dower house on the property. Several Hawks have settled not too far away, however. The countess is thinking about having a few of them here for a celebration of Christmas. What do you think? Will you stay here for the holiday?"

Christmas was two weeks away but the thought of returning to Ralston House for the holiday held little appeal.

"I believe Violet would enjoy it," he said.

"But not you?"

Victor bristled under the earl's close scrutiny. "I would very much enjoy it, Gabriel. Thank you for the invitation."

Gabriel blinked. "Good God, you're prickly."

"I don't know what you're—"

"Please don't take offense," Gabriel cut in, holding up his hand. "It's not my place to pry, but you seem wound a bit tight."

Victor gave a slight nod. "I admit I've had a hard time of it."

"The curse, you mean?"

Victor's head snapped up and he met the earl's gaze. Knowledge and kinship was there in their dark depths. "Yes," he choked out.

Gabriel looked thoughtful for a moment, then spoke. "I used to fuck my staff, too."

Victor stiffened. "How did you know?"

"We're Hawks, Victor. You can't be much different than any of the rest of us. The beast demands satisfaction, and you don't seem the kind to ride about the county fucking the peasantry."

"No. The notion is abhorrent."

The earl shrugged. "Then who else would you fuck?"

His cheeks felt hot again.

"Not your lovely third cousin?" Gabriel asked in a low voice.

"Not if I can help it," Victor vowed.

Gabriel was silent for a moment. "Well, if any of my staff is willing, you may take your pleasure where you find it."

"Will that help, do you think? My own staff surely hasn't."

"With the curse?" At Victor's nod Gabriel shook his head. "I'm afraid not. I've found only one cure, though it seems to work for more than just myself."

Victor could guess his meaning. "Marriage? Forgive me, but Hawks don't marry."

"Oh we do, Victor. But it's not marriage precisely that does the trick."

"What, then?"

Gabriel shook his head again. "I don't think you're ready to hear the answer, quite frankly. I suppose I'll see you at dinner?"

It was as close to a dismissal as Victor had ever heard but he didn't take any offense. If the earl's holdings were a tenth as vast as Victor supposed, the man must be very busy.

He stood then, bowing his head. "I thank you again, Gabriel, and look forward to getting to know your family during this visit."

Gabriel smiled and Victor doubted he himself had ever looked that happy in his life. He left the study, bound for a maid or footman to show him to his guest room.

Victor couldn't fault his host for not divulging what had broken the bonds of his Hawk beast. Not really. Who was Victor to him, besides a newly met relative who shared his looks and his curse?

He thought about Violet then, settling into her guest room no doubt quite far from his. At least he would have Cabot the footman for company at some point. Again, that surge of desire struck him.

How could he be attracted to two people? One, a girl he'd known far too long and the other a man he'd only just set eyes on?

And he was to spend Christmas here at Hawksfell. He had to admit a thread of excitement wound through his resignation. His mother always made Christmas something special for her only child. He'd missed that, first as she'd fallen sick and then as he'd anticipated a sad holiday this year.

He was glad he'd brought Violet to Hawksfell, if only for the holiday. She deserved to have some happiness. He never should have touched her last night. Hell, he never should have let her touch him!

God, she'd been sweet in her release and so determined to please him. His cock hardened when he thought of her wrapping those delicate fingers around his shaft. She wasn't meant for him, though. Neither were any of the earl's able and willing staff, his attraction to Cabot notwithstanding.

Maybe he'd figure out how to break his curse himself. Because he was damned if he'd hurt Violet or anyone else with his dark Hawk desires.

Chapter 4

"Christmas!" Violet exclaimed. "Oh, how lovely!"

Lady Hawksfell smiled at her from across the table. "Gabriel told me of what happened recently at Ralston House, Violet."

Violet's heart skipped a beat before she realized what the countess meant. She couldn't know about the pleasures Violet and Victor had shared. She was clearly speaking about Victor's poor mother.

"We were saddened by Victor's mother's passing," Violet said.

"And that's why we believe celebrating here with us and a flock of Hawks will be just the thing," Michael Crowley put in.

Violet nodded to the handsome blond man seated to the countess's right. He'd been introduced as her third cousin and the two of them were very alike in looks. He seemed friendly and warm and it was obvious both Lady and Lord Hawksfell were fond of him.

"I'm grateful for the inclusion," Violet said.

"I daresay Victor wouldn't want to be without you," Michael said.

Her gaze shot to where Victor sat, the usual look of dour detachment on his handsome face. Were anyone to consider him at the moment, they would have more than a little trouble believing he would ever miss her.

"Isn't that true, Victor?" Lady Hawksfell asked.

Victor blinked his long lashes and faced the countess. "Forgive me, Lady Hawksfell. Did you ask me something?"

She flashed a dazzling smile. "Millicent, please. And yes, we were speaking about the holiday."

Victor smiled, a small expression that sent a shock through Violet nevertheless. She just couldn't look at him another moment. A footman appeared at her side to take away her empty plate and she glanced up, grateful for the diversion. She was immediately seized by the gorgeous blue depths of his eyes.

"Are you finished, miss?" he asked.

She stared up at his beautiful face, intrigued when his sculpted lips parted. Her mind worked. What had he asked her? Oh, yes. Her plate.

"Y–yes, thank you," she managed to say.

He took her plate and stood. My, he was tall. And broad-shouldered. Conversation continued around the table, mostly dominated by the countess and her cousin, but she couldn't help but compare Victor to this blond god. They were very different in looks. Victor was so strong and dark and this footman was lean and light. She'd given Victor pleasure. Seen his handsome face intense as his climax took him. What would this pretty man look like in his release?

Her body flushed and she dipped her head so no one would notice her blush. Why was she thinking about this stranger in such a manner? It was enough that she was often consumed with thoughts of Victor and his passions. Now she was lusting after this poor footman?

When the group rose from the table and went into the main hall to retire to the parlor she begged off.

"I'm afraid I feel a bit of a headache coming on," she said to Lady Hawksfell.

"Oh, dear." The countess put a hand on Violet's arm. "Go rest, Violet. I daresay we have plenty of time ahead of us to enjoy the coming holiday."

Violet nodded, grateful for the ease of her escape.

"Will you be able to find your way to your room, Miss Ralston?" the earl asked her.

She blinked at him. Would she? The manor was enormous. "I…"

"Cabot, please show Miss Ralston to her guest room," he said.

"Of course," the handsome footman she'd fantasized about answered with a bow. His voice was smooth and melodious, a perfect fit for his good looks.

Her cheeks heated as she followed him up the stairs to her room. A glance over her shoulder showed her that Victor watched her, his dark eyes intent. Was he thinking about last night as well? Did he want to discover if more could be between them than pleasure from their hands? She'd discovered that the servants' gossip had been correct regarding the size of his manhood. Were they right about his intensity as well?

As Cabot led her down the hallway to her room a disturbing thought struck her. Would Victor avail himself on the servants here at Hawksfell? There were certainly plenty of them, handsome men and pretty maids to tempt him. The girl, Ivy, sent to help her was very pretty indeed. She sniffed as tears threatened. Cabot stilled outside of her door.

"Are you all right, miss?" he asked.

She lifted her chin, gathering up her tangled emotions as she tried to present an expression of quiet dignity. "Yes, Cabot. Thank you."

He didn't look convinced. His brows were draw together as he regarded her with solemn eyes. "You seem upset."

She waved a hand and walked into the guest room. "I suppose I'm just lamenting the loss of something I never had."

He followed and tilted his head to the side, a slight smile curving one corner of his lovely mouth. "Forgive me, but that sounds a bit maudlin."

She smiled in return. "Yes. I have been known to be that."

Staring up into Cabot's eyes, she felt the floor shift. Her body swayed toward him, pulled by his remarkable looks and incredible scent. Where Victor smelled and tasted dark and spiced this man's scent was hot and fresh. Would he taste that way as well?

"I'm all right, Cabot," she said, giving him a small smile. "I'm afraid I've kept you from your duties."

To her astonishment, he glanced out into the hallway, then closed the door. He faced her again and his smile widened as he tipped his head toward hers. Oh, he was all smooth charm and beauty, but she couldn't form the words to send him from her room.

"My duties sometimes involve helping a damsel in distress, miss." His voice caressed her every nerve, making her flush hot and cold.

Her breath caught. "Cabot..."

His mouth came close to hers, his full lips so near she could smell his minty breath. She parted her lips and rose up on her tiptoes to press her mouth to his. Electricity shot through her, the sensation so like her reaction to Victor's kiss her eyes drifted closed. As she opened her mouth she felt his tongue probe inside. He was delicious.

A soft moan escaped her and he echoed the sound. Then he jerked away from her. "Forgive me, miss," he rushed out, his voice low.

She opened her eyes to see his cheeks had gone pink. Taken with his dilated pupils, the effect on her was remarkable despite the space he put between them. He looked good enough to eat and, despite the delectable meal served by the manor to its guests, she was suddenly ravenous.

"There is nothing to forgive," she breathed, pressing so close to him he backed up against the door.

He placed his hands on her shoulders and held her from him. "I could lose my position."

She felt a rush of power course through her. Not the power to make this man lose his job but the power to tempt him to put everything at risk to kiss her. She had to taste him again.

"Kiss me, Cabot."

He licked his lips and her body flushed again. With a soft sound of defeat, he crushed his mouth to hers. She reached up to grab onto his shoulders. His tongue drove into her mouth again and she couldn't help but rub hers against it. He pulled back just a hairsbreadth and cursed softly. Then his tongue trailed over her throat and she leaned her head back. He licked the hollow of her throat and she shivered as her nipples grew tight in her corset.

"You smell incredible," he rasped as he cupped her bottom. His teeth nipped at her bosom. "Like sweet wildflowers."

She could feel the length of his shaft against her, and the memory of being held this close by Victor crashed over her. Her woman's flesh swelled and she felt her drawers go damp.

"Oh, Cabot!" She pressed closer to him still. "Touch me."

He brought one shaking hand to her breast and gently squeezed. Sharp pleasure stabbed through her as her nipples grew even harder.

"You're a package, Miss Ralston."

"Violet," she said on a breath. "My name is violet."

He stilled, then laughed softly. "Fitting."

She tried to reason through his words but she couldn't. "What?"

He brought his brow to hers. "You smell like violets."

She laughed. "Cabot."

He smiled, then straightened his livery. His jacket was crumpled and his tie askew. "I must get back downstairs, miss."

"You just had your hands on my bottom, Cabot. You may call me Violet."

He flushed again, all signs of the smooth flirt gone. He wore a look of hunger in his beautiful blue eyes yet his lips were set in a tight determined line. Oh, how many times had she seen that very combination etched on Victor's beloved face?

"Go," she said, hoping she sounded calm and worldly. "We'll talk again."

He bowed his head and opened the door, then hurried down the hall with smooth strides. She watched him for a long moment, then closed the door. Sagging against the wood panel, she squeezed her eyes shut. Shame washed over her.

How could she give herself to a man she'd just met? True, he was very pretty and affected her much like Victor did. As amazing as that should be, she wanted him as much as she did Victor.

"Victor," she sobbed, her eyes stinging with tears.

She'd never been more confused in her life. And she was staying here at Hawksfell Manor until Christmas! How was she going to withstand the chill of Victor's indifference and the heat of Cabot's interest?

"Happy Christmas to me," she murmured.

* * * *

"What the hell was I thinking?" Cabot muttered as he ascended the stairs to his attic room.

"About what?" Ivy asked.

Cabot froze and took a calming breath. He turned his head and saw that Ivy leaned against the wall beside his door with an expectant look on her face. He didn't need her teasing and flirtation at the moment. He was still at sixes and sevens over his wild attraction to Miss Violet Ralston.

"Good evening, Ivy," he said, his voice cool.

Ivy toyed with her hair, which was now in a loose twist set over her shoulder. "I've been waiting for you."

He knew in that instant he could pull her into his room and fuck her like mad if he wanted to. She wouldn't put up one bit of protest. He was still semi-hard from kissing the lovely Violet, yet he didn't have the slightest desire for this hungry girl, no matter the circumstances or her willingness.

"Then I'm afraid you're going to be disappointed," he said.

She pouted then. "Oh, Cabot! You're cruel."

He opened his door and pushed past her into his room. "I don't know what you mean."

He went to the mirror set atop his chest of drawers and saw that he didn't quite look like the impeccable servant Mr. Carstairs liked to present to staff and guests. No, his hair was mussed and his jacket a mess of creases. Lovely. Now he'd have to change before going upstairs to see to Baron Ralston. He had to see to the baron's fire as well as ready his clothes for tomorrow, all the while trying not to think about his indulgence with the man's cousin.

He shrugged out of his jacket and heard Ivy gasp. Glancing over his shoulder, he saw she'd entered and was now staring at his groin. He guessed she could see that his cock tented his trousers from this angle.

"If you'll be so kind as to leave my room," he stated.

At last the girl seemed to remember herself. "Oh, I'm sorry!"

Her cheeks were red as she backed out of his room. She closed the door with a bang and he winced. At least he could count on Mr. Carstairs and Mrs. Holmes being down in the servants' hall at this hour. He'd fucked half the staff over the past two years and knew just when the time was right for a romp without risk of discovery.

He shook out his jacket and decided it wasn't too worse for wear. No doubt the baron would send for him soon, but Cabot wanted to anticipate his needs. Serving guests well would put him in good stead at the manor, and there was something about this particular Hawk guest that left him feeling unsettled.

Lord Ralston was a handsome devil, as all the Hawks were. He might be third cousin to the lovely Violet but there was no resemblance that Cabot could see. He had a graceful way of moving though. And those lovely dark Hawk eyes. His demeanor seemed quite different from the last few to visit the manor, however. He was quiet and removed, despite the longing looks his cousin gave him. No, Cabot hadn't missed that woman's hunger either. Ivy's coquettish expressions paled by comparison. It was like nothing he'd seen before, and when she'd turned that wanting gaze up at him like that in her room he'd simply had to kiss her.

"Rutting fool," he chided himself.

Once more put together, he left his room and went down toward the bachelor wing. As he neared the room given to this latest visitor, he heard a groaning from within. It was low and deep, almost sensual, and sent awareness over his body.

He rapped and pushed open the door, stunned to find Baron Ralston stripped to the waist. He was beautifully built, so strong and broad and sculpted. His shoulders were tense and he was holding himself stiff.

"My lord?" Cabot asked softly, closing the door behind him.

Lord Ralston jerked, then turned slightly. Cabot's breath caught. His chest was lovely as well but it was what was in one of his large hands that sent Cabot's pulse pounding. Lord Ralston was holding his long, thick Hawk cock, and Cabot had never seen a more impressive one in his life.

Chapter 5

Victor stared at the footman now closed in his room with him. His pretty blue eyes were fastened on his cock. There was no denying his interest, and his shaft grew longer.

"Cabot?" he asked, his voice rough to his own ears.

"Y–yes, my lord." Cabot raised his gaze from his cock to his face. "Are you all right?"

Victor hissed out a breath as he tried to stuff his cock back into his trousers. Every movement was excruciating now. "I'm fine," he bit out.

For a split second he thought the footman was going to take him at his word. Then he stepped closer, an expression of sympathy on his face.

"Forgive me, but you are not fine." Cabot touched his bare shoulder, the gesture comforting and sensual at the same time. "You are in a bad way."

Victor released his cock and fisted his hands at his sides. "You've worked here for some time, I take it?"

Cabot nodded. "Two years."

He met Cabot's eyes. "You served the earl?"

Cabot blinked long lashes before recognition filled his gaze. Heat flared in those blue eyes. God, he reminded Victor of Violet in that moment.

"I have," Cabot said, his voice low. He reached out and grasped Victor's cock, stroking gently. "I can serve you."

Victor shook his head. "That's not required. I didn't mean to make any such demand."

Cabot smiled, his full lips curving in a way that made Victor long to kiss him. He'd never kissed a man. Hell, he'd never kissed anyone but Violet.

"You didn't demand anything, my lord."

His hand moved faster now and Victor leaned back against the dressing table. "God, that feels so damn good."

"How long has it been?" Cabot asked.

"I'm not like my other Hawk relatives, Cabot. I try not to fuck that often."

Cabot stilled, then shook his head. "That is a shame."

"I find release." Victor moaned as Cabot's thumb teased the slit on his cock's head. "In a maid's mouth. Sometimes with a groom."

"But you can't use your own hand." It wasn't a question. Cabot must know quite a bit about the Hawk's curse.

Victor shook his head. "No, I can't. The last time I came was with…"

He all but bit his tongue. Couldn't speak of Violet and ruin her reputation. God, her release had been remarkable and the memory of her enthusiasm when she stroked his cock was what had him so damn hard tonight.

"The last time you came was with her?" Cabot asked.

Victor opened his eyes and saw knowledge stamped on Cabot's features. The man somehow knew he meant Violet.

Victor bit his lip, then nodded. "I didn't fuck her," he said. "I wanted to but I didn't."

"She's gorgeous. It's no wonder you're hard for her."

"That is plain speaking, Cabot." He let his gaze trail over the handsome footman. His cock was clearly hard in his pants. "And who is that cock hard for, may I ask?"

Cabot continued to stroke him. "For her," he admitted on a whisper.

"For her?" he asked, his mind trying to make sense of things. "Miss Ralston?"

Cabot nodded. "She's beautiful. I…kissed her."

Victor pictured Cabot holding Violet close and lust washed over him. "You kissed her?"

"Yes. She was upset and…" He shrugged.

"I know why she was upset," Victor muttered.

"She wants you, I believe," Cabot said. "I completely understand why."

It was Victor's turn to blink his confusion. "What?"

"I admitted that my cock is hard for her, Lord Ralston." His eyes sparkled as he leaned closer. "But it's also hard for you."

Then he brought his lips to Victor's. Victor's shock gave way to pleasure as Cabot kissed him. His taste was fresh and hot and he cupped his head and drove his tongue into his mouth. Cabot moaned, returning his kiss expertly as his hand continued to work him. Victor thrust against his hand and closed his eyes again.

Victor pulled away slightly, his breath coming fast. "Please. I have to come."

"Do you want to fuck me, my lord?" Cabot asked, his voice laced with desire.

Victor gave a shaky nod. "I do."

Cabot smiled against his lips and stepped back to strip out of his livery. The man was beautiful, all lithe muscles and golden skin. As he stripped off his trousers Victor sucked in a breath. The man's cock was long and thick, nearly as large as his damned Hawk cock.

"You're very pretty, Cabot," he managed to say.

Cabot shrugged a graceful shoulder, obviously fully aware of just how handsome he was in and out of clothes. For the first time in his life, Victor was seized with the urge to touch another besides Violet. He wanted to stroke and pet Cabot and then fuck his ass until they both came.

"Turn around," he growled.

Cabot grinned and turned, bracing his hands on the dressing table. Victor allowed himself to feel as he ran his hands over Cabot's hot skin. He was smoothly muscled and built like a Roman statue. Cupping his ass, he felt Cabot tense and then let out a sigh.

"I *want* to fuck you," Victor said, bemused.

Cabot glanced at him over his shoulder. "I realize that," he teased.

Victor shook his head. "No, Cabot. I want this, not just need this."

Cabot nodded solemnly. "Then take me, my lord."

"Call me Victor, Cabot." As he fingered Cabot's hole, they both shuddered. "You're not serving me."

"Mmm," Cabot murmured. "Victor, then."

Victor looked down at his cock as he thrust between Cabot's cheeks. "I'm afraid I'll hurt you."

Cabot arched toward him. "There is a jar of cream in the top drawer," he said on a moan.

Victor reached around him to pull the drawer open. A jar did sit inside, and he grabbed it. "It seems the last Hawk to visit used this room?"

"The last several, Victor."

"You didn't..."

Cabot shook his head, his thick blond hair falling over his forehead. "No."

Victor opened the jar and dipped two fingers inside. The cream smelled like soap and flowers, a pleasant combination. He set the jar back down on the dressing table and put his hands on Cabot once again. Easing two fingers inside him, he felt the tightness and couldn't wait to feel it around his cock. He'd never craved a man before and the sensation was heady indeed.

"Cabot," he said on a whisper, bringing his lips to the other man's ear. "Take all of me."

"God, yes," Cabot groaned. "Fuck me, Victor."

It was all the permission Victor needed. He positioned himself at his hole and sank slowly inside. Cabot was stock still and Victor was trembling, then they both began to move.

Holding on to Cabot's narrow hips, Victor thrust in and out. They were both moaning now and Victor knew he wouldn't last long. Cabot gripped the table in front of him, throwing his head back to rest on Victor's shoulder.

Victor moved to capture Cabot's lips as he continued to drive into him. He could feel his orgasm start, his balls tightening until he lost his control.

"I'm coming," he groaned, wrapping an arm around Cabot's chest and holding him closer.

Cabot let out a breath as he arched, wrapping a hand around his own cock as Victor came hard inside him. His heart was pounding, his blood rushing in his ears, but he managed to reach around and cover Cabot's fingers with his own. Together they stroked until Cabot shuddered against him and climaxed.

Their breathing was harsh and Victor had to brace his feet apart to keep from collapsing over Cabot on the dressing table. He'd never felt such pleasure except from Violet's hand, and certainly never felt the connection he inexplicably felt with Cabot tonight. For the first time, crushing guilt didn't choke him after fucking. No, he was released from his beast and could breathe again.

"Cabot," he said softly, kissing his fevered cheek. "That was remarkable."

Cabot nodded, licking his lips as his breathing slowed. "You know how to ride, my lord."

Victor withdrew from Cabot and tucked his sated cock back into his trousers. "Victor, Cabot. You agreed."

Cabot withdrew a handkerchief and wiped the table and then himself before turning to face Victor. "In this room, I'll call you Victor."

Relief washed over him. "I don't want to lose this connection, Cabot."

Cabot dressed quickly, then faced him. "What are you saying?"

Victor brushed a hand through his hair and shrugged. "I want to have you again."

Cabot smiled, all smooth charm, and Victor felt the impact of the man's attraction. "I'm pleased." His expression sobered and Victor once more saw the man behind the charm. "But what are you going to do about her?"

Victor thought about Violet and knew his need for her was still burning inside of him. He'd surrendered and taken Cabot but he still wanted Violet.

Victor let out a sigh. "I have no idea."

Cabot put a hand on his bare shoulder. "You want her."

Victor nodded.

"And you want me?" Cabot asked.

Victor met his blue eyes so like Violet's. "Yes."

Cabot grinned now. "Then you shall have us both."

Amazingly, Victor felt a laugh bubble up inside him. "How?"

"You're not the only one who wants two here, Victor."

Victor's mouth dropped open. "She wants you, too?"

"Of course."

Victor did laugh then. And he felt lighter than he ever had before.

* * * *

Violet walked about the frozen grounds of Hawksfell Manor, her nerves in a tangle. Last night had been astonishing on several levels. When the Hawks all spoke of the coming holiday with such warm anticipation, she'd so wanted to fit in and celebrate with them. The long year caring for Victor's mother hadn't left time or energy for celebrating and Victor's prickly demeanor made any notion of bringing up the subject to him ridiculous. She'd seen the longing in his eyes, however. It nearly broke her heart that he kept himself as removed from these people as much as he always had from her.

Turning up the collar of her coat, she made her way around toward the back of the manor house. Hawksfell was enormous, but she'd spotted an outbuilding. She assumed it was a garage or carriage house, and considered hiding out in it until dinnertime arrived again. Breakfast had been quiet, as the earl and his family had gone off to the village. At least she wouldn't have to make conversation with the absurdly happy Lady Hawksfell and her undeniably pleasant cousin. If the earl was seeing to business he'd been considerate enough to take them along with him today.

Victor hadn't been present but neither had Cabot the footman, thank goodness. Oh, the way she'd shamed herself with him!

He had been so kind to her, though. And he was so very attractive. His kisses were sweet and hot, and on this cold morning she believed they might be just the thing to warm her.

Shivering from the combination of the chill of the air and the heat of her thoughts, she turned back toward the house. A maid took her coat when she entered. Violet rubbed her bare hands together as she headed toward the library. She'd taken note of it this morning as she'd passed toward the breakfast room, and it was as good a place to be alone as any other she could find. She was an expert on being alone, of course.

She took a book from one of the shelves without giving it much thought and settled in a chair beside the well-tended fire. She was soon warm and a little drowsy, holding the closed book in her lap as she stared out the nearest window at the white winter landscape beyond.

What would happen after the holiday? After she and Victor returned to Ralston House? There was truly no place for her there, despite his familial kindness toward her. She had no one else to turn to. She would end up an old maid, haunting Ralston after Victor inevitably wed and brought his wife home. A stab of pain shot through her heart at the mere thought of him giving another what she longed for from him. Passion, yes. But she wanted him to take the freedom to touch her when he wished to. To take the pleasure she offered as more than a release of his Hawk lusts. To love her and no other woman!

"It can never be," she whispered, her throat tight.

"And what is that, miss?" a man's voice inquired from the doorway.

She blinked at Cabot, leaning against the jamb and looking for all the world like a man of leisure despite his impeccable livery. "Cabot."

He smiled in that way that sent shivers over her body and entered the room. To her surprise he closed the door behind him with a click and faced her again. "Ah, Violet."

She nearly melted at his smooth utterance of her name. She licked her lips, longing for another taste of his kisses. Still, propriety must be observed.

"What are you about, Cabot?"

He stepped closer and she caught his scent. "I could ask you the same."

She mirrored his smile. "Impertinent this afternoon, I see. You have a saucy tongue."

He shrugged. "I seem to recall you enjoyed my tongue just last evening."

Her cheeks went as hot as the fire behind the grate. She couldn't deny his words. She'd tasted her fill and loved what he'd done to her during that brief madness in her guest room.

"I did," she admitted on a whisper. "Very much."

His blue eyes sparkled with intent as he bent over her. She was forced to crane her neck to meet his gaze. He was nearly as tall as Victor, after all.

"Do you wish to know more of what my saucy tongue can do?"

Her mouth dropped open even as it began to water. Her nipples pinched tight in her corset and she shuddered. "W–what, precisely, can it do?"

He brought his mouth to her ear and gave her earlobe a lick. "It can taste you all over." He nibbled on the cord of her neck and laughed softly. "It can delve into your pussy and see if it's as sweet as your lips."

Her drawers grew wet as she imagined such a thing. "Never say you wish to lick me...there."

He nodded, then met her eyes with his. "I could eat you for hours, Violet." He shivered and blew out a breath. "The mere thought of it makes me hard."

She glanced down at the front of his trousers. She could make out the shape and length of his manhood through the fine fabric and realized he must be as affected as Victor was, curse or no. The night before they'd left Ralston House she'd felt Victor's desire and he'd touched hers. But what Cabot was suggesting couldn't be possible.

"Victor touched me," she rushed out, her eyes drifting closed with embarrassment and remembrance. "With only his hand."

Cabot smiled again. "And you came, didn't you?"

"Came?" She pondered the word, then realized what it meant. That mind-shattering pleasure Victor had given her with his long, strong fingers. That climax that had shocked and thrilled her to her toes. "Oh. Y–yes."

"I can make you come with my mouth, Violet."

She gripped the arms of her chair, her eyes opening wide. "You can?"

He nodded, then straightened again. "But believe me, the library isn't the place."

She glanced past his handsome face and realized she'd forgotten where they were. Her body was aching, her pulse pounding, just from his words. She'd never be able to hold back her screams should he touch her. Oh, how she wanted him to touch her!

"Where?" she asked breathlessly. "Cabot, where can you make me...come?"

He just grinned and took her hand in his.

Chapter 6

Violet followed behind Cabot as he wound his way through the great house. He seemed to know every vacant hallway and unoccupied chamber on the way toward the stairs, for they never encountered any other staff. At the top of the stairs he turned away from the family bedrooms.

"Where are you taking me?" she asked.

He glanced back over his shoulder, his full lips agape. "Taking you? God, I wish I could take you."

She realized what she'd said and bit her lip. He groaned softly and quickly kissed her.

"We're bound for the bachelor's wing," he said.

"The bachelor's wing?" That was where Victor was ensconced, and no one else at present to her knowledge. Cabot had picked the perfect trysting spot for certain.

He stopped before a closed door and faced her, placing his hands on her shoulders. "You're certain?"

Was she certain she was going to tryst with this man? This warm, caring man who made her feel things only Victor had before? But Victor was far and gone from her forever. That was certain. And Cabot stood before her with an expression of concern on his handsome face. His fair brows were furrowed and, even though his cheeks were ruddy with his own desires, she was sure that if she cried off he would honor her wishes. That realization was enough to make her decision.

Before she could do more than nod, he opened the door and ushered her inside. It was a beautifully decorated room, done in shades of blue. That was all she noticed at the moment, for Cabot took off his jacket and ran his hands over her. He was beautifully built. She could see that through his fine linen shirt. As he drew her close she could feel the muscles in his chest and arms working.

"You are such a delectable bundle, Violet." He unbuttoned her dress and stared down at her corset. "My, my."

Her breasts were all but spilling over the top of it and she ached for him to put his saucy tongue on her flesh. "Cabot, please."

He spun her around and quickly worked the hooks until the corset fell to the floor around her ankles. She covered her breasts with her hands but when he gently tugged them away along with the thin straps of her chemise. She surprised herself by letting him look his fill.

"As pretty as a flower." He cupped one breast and dragged his thumb over its aching nipple. "I wager your pussy will be as pretty."

Her knees were weak as he drew her closer. Closing his mouth over the nipple, he began to toy with her other breast. His arm was strong around her as he backed her toward the bed. She felt it at her backside and let herself sink down. His mouth never ceased its magic, his tongue teasing and his teeth nibbling. Sparks of pleasure coursed through her, making her ache for more.

"Taste me everywhere, Cabot," she sighed.

He lifted his head and winked at her. "Who has the saucy tongue now?"

She giggled and leaned back on her elbows. "Me?"

"You."

He lifted the hem of her chemise to her waist and spread her legs wide. The room was warm and her body hotter still, yet she shivered as he removed her drawers. His eyes ran over her bared flesh and she felt herself swell.

"Oh, you have a very pretty pussy," he said, his voice thick.

Then he kissed her there. He made a sound of delight as he licked her. Collapsing beneath him, she closed her eyes and gave herself over to his expertise.

"You're very good at this, Cabot."

He made a sound, then inserted a finger into her. "I've never tasted such a delectable pussy, Violet. You're sweeter than I'd imagined."

She couldn't hold a thought as his finger moved inside of her. His tongue circled that very spot Victor had touched before and she felt a lifting of her body as she began an ascent toward climax again. "Make me come!" she cried. "Oh, Cabot!"

He licked and sucked as he worked her, and stars lit behind her eyelids. Spreading herself wider, she surrendered and cried out as her orgasm took her.

Cabot came up and kissed her as she caught her breath. A lock of his golden hair lay over his forehead and his blue eyes were dark. "Have I pleased you?"

She stared at him, her body weak and her heartbeat erratic. He'd pleased her as promised and it surpassed her fevered imaginings. Not since that night with Victor had she felt such pleasure. The memory stabbed at her and she sucked in a breath. Inexplicably, her eyes stung with tears and she squeezed them shut. "Yes," she sobbed.

Cabot was silent above her.

"You don't *sound* pleased," another man's voice intoned.

She opened her eyes to find Victor standing over the bed. Her legs were still wide open and Cabot was stretched over her nearly naked body. A flush of embarrassment spread over her body. "Victor!"

He shrugged out of his jacket as Cabot had done, tossing it toward the chair set near the window.

"You'll wrinkle it," Cabot intoned, leaning up on his elbows.

Victor lifted a shoulder. "My valet shall attend to it."

Cabot laughed and rolled off of her gracefully to stand on the other side of the bed. Violet blinked rapidly. This was all so odd, the two of them here and Victor almost teasing Cabot.

"Am I dreaming?" she murmured.

Victor shook his head. He still wore his usual dark expression but there was something else there in his face. That hunger she'd seen before.

"Were you actually teasing Cabot just then?" she asked.

"Turnabout is fair play, Violet," he said, his voice smooth. "He was just, um, teasing you."

His dark gaze fell on her pussy and she felt a rekindling of the passion Cabot had raised. Oh, she was shameless!

She brought her thighs together and sat up on the bed. Her wrinkled chemise made a poor covering but she gathered it in front of her breasts just the same. "I don't know what to say."

He continued to remove his clothes. "I'm tired of my vow, Violet. I'm tired of being alone when I want you so much."

The fervency of his words was unexpected. "You want me?"

His gaze was intent. "Of course."

"But I've just let Cabot…"

To her amazement, Victor nodded. "I saw what you just let Cabot do." His eyes raked over her. "I've pictured your pretty pussy many times but I admit it surpasses my imaginings. I long for a taste of you as well."

"Now I know I'm dreaming." She managed to rise and stood at the foot of the bed. Victor stripped off his shirt and she was momentarily stunned speechless by the sight of his magnificent chest. It was a bit broader than Cabot's, swirled with dark hairs and ridged in all the right places. She swallowed. "What are you about, Victor?"

"I'm going to forget myself," he said, his voice low. "I'm going to give in and take you at last."

She shook her head, backing away from him. "What does this mean?" Her stomach sank as a horrible thought struck her. "Oh, you believe that since I allowed Cabot to give me pleasure—"

"You're welcome," Cabot cut in, laughter in his voice.

She waved a hand at him. "You believe that I shall allow you to take me? In exchange for what?"

A pained expression crossed Victor's face and her heart clenched.

"I don't have anything to offer," he rasped. "Just myself, in this moment."

His breathing was labored and she longed to draw him into her arms. Cabot might have made her body sing but Victor made her heart ache. She'd longed for him forever. This was her only chance to learn about passion from Cabot and, just perhaps, be enough to keep Victor's beast at bay when they returned to their odd, removed existence at Ralston House. She would never have his heart but perhaps having his passion would be enough.

Taking a deep breath, she surrendered as she had for Cabot.

"Take me, Victor," she whispered.

* * * *

Victor couldn't help but stare at this girl he'd known forever, in passing for years and more intimately over the past several months. Violet was a pretty thing, but flushed with passion as she was now? She was damned gorgeous. Her hair was a tangled mess, golden curls resting over her smooth shoulders and trailing down toward her pert backside. Her legs were shapely and her breasts were round and full and his mouth watered for a taste of her deep pink nipples.

When Cabot proposed this plan, he'd been intrigued. When Violet accompanied the man to his guest room, he'd been stunned. And now that he'd watched Cabot lick and taste her incredible body? He was so hard he wanted to throw his head back and howl to the heavens.

Instead, he made himself approach her slowly. He could smell her flowery scent, hot and intoxicating. She was aroused. Her pupils were dilated and her eyes had darkened nearly to purple. Out of the corner of his eye he noticed that Cabot stepped back from the bed. Dragging his eyes away from Violet's delectable form, he flicked his gaze fully to Cabot. The man was smiling as he lifted his chin in encouragement.

He turned to Violet again. "You're certain, Violet?" he asked. "If you say no, I'll not judge you."

Her thick lashes fluttered as she gazed up at him. "You won't judge me? Not even after what I've just done?"

He took her trembling hands in his, pulling her closer. "I would never be so callous."

Her full lips parted, then she shook her head. "Kiss me, Victor."

He brought his mouth to hers and began to taste her. She tasted a bit of Cabot, but that could be his lingering scent on her skin. The combination of the man he'd recently fucked and the girl he was going to drove him wild. "Easy," he growled.

She pulled back a hairsbreadth. "What did you say?"

He kissed her lips again, then dropped his head to the side of her neck. "I was telling myself to go easy, Violet. I'm afraid I want to strip off what little clothing you have on and fuck you. Hard."

She trembled and pressed closer to him. "Oh, my."

He could hear the sound of a cough and knew Cabot was stifling a chuckle. It should almost be ridiculous but his cock felt so full and hard for Violet it was like it was his first time. Like he hadn't fucked the servants at Ralston House for years and Cabot just last night.

Dropping his hands from her, he stepped back and unfastened his trousers. The warmth of the air in the room made his balls ache. He hissed through his teeth as his cock grew harder. His beast was wild for her and he knew he had to take care.

"Place her on the bed, Cabot," he said.

Cabot nodded and gathered Violet in his arms. "Come, sweetheart. Trust me, you're in for quite a ride."

She looked from Cabot to himself, then swallowed audibly. "Oh, my," she said again.

Victor found a small smile for that. Cabot's fingers were deft as they removed her chemise and she was soon spread and ready for him. Praying for the presence of mind to restrain himself, he climbed onto the bed and covered her with his naked body.

Her nipples were hard against his chest, and her mound pressed up against his cock. He'd never taken a woman this way, touching her with every inch of his body. When her arms twined around his neck, her nails biting into his shoulders, he clenched his teeth against the shout of excitement that fought to escape him.

"Ah, Violet," he moaned, burying his face between her breasts.

Her scent was heavier here, and when he flicked his tongue over her nipple he could taste her sweetness. Delving between her thighs with one hand, he stroked her pussy. She was wet, from Cabot's attentions and from her fresh arousal. With two fingers inside of her, he could feel the proof of her virginity. That, and how tight she was. It was going to be a close thing. His cock was huge and his need greater than he'd ever felt before. He tried to ready her for his assault, and as he moved his fingers in and out of her she began to purr and writhe beneath him.

"Yes, Victor," she sighed. "Please..."

When she bit her lip again he nearly came on her soft belly. Shifting, he forced himself to slow as he positioned his cock at her pussy. Her flesh scalded him, made him ache to spill inside her.

A glance at Cabot showed him watching avidly, his cheeks flushed and his eyes sparkling. Apparently he was enjoying this as much as Victor had enjoyed watching Cabot lick her. It was passing strange but he supposed there was a connection among the three of them now.

He looked back down at her beautiful face. "I'm sorry if this hurts," he said. Then he drove inside her hot cunt with one deep thrust.

She cried out in obvious pain and he held himself still.

"Violet, Violet," he said, taking measured breaths.

She sobbed, but there was an edge to her cries. A piercing of want that stunned him.

"Oh, take me!" she shouted, clutching more tightly at his shoulders.

He blinked, then began to move. Her hips rose to meet him and he was soon pounding into her hard and fast. Their bodies were coated with sweat and he lifted her legs up around his waist.

"My God," he groaned, feeling every inch of her grasp his shaft. "Oh, my God."

She began to sob again, her body arching wildly beneath him. She shattered then, coming tight around his shaft as he continued to ride her. He couldn't do anything else but buck and thrust until he felt his own climax start.

"Violet, let me…" he began, bracing himself on his hands to withdraw.

She drew him closer in the throes of her orgasm and he suddenly came with a groan, pouring his seed deep inside of her in hot spurts that nearly turned him inside out.

He took in great gasps of air as he struggled to hold himself off her slight form. Her head was turned to the side, her eyes closed as she took ragged breaths through her parted lips. Her pussy still held him tight, aftershocks of pleasure tickling at him as he squeezed his own eyes shut at last.

The feel of her, the scent of her and their sex all around them, was something he knew he'd never forget. And, like his time with Cabot last night, he didn't feel the wash of cold shame that he was so used to following his climax. He couldn't think about what that meant at the moment, however. He was just too bloody satisfied.

"Violet," he said finally, opening his eyes again and bringing his brow to hers. "Are you all right?"

She shifted and gazed up at him. "Oh, yes."

Cabot did laugh then, slapping Victor's shoulder. "Well done, Victor."

Victor barked out a surprised chuckle and shook his head.

Chapter 7

Cabot helped her dress as Victor pulled on his trousers. The matter of her remarkable hair was beyond Cabot's expertise, apparently. She kept her eyes diverted as she fussed at the golden curls. With a breath, she dropped her hands to her sides.

"I suppose I'll see you at dinner, Victor?" she asked, her voice small.

"Of course," he answered dumbly.

She seemed so vulnerable poised there and somehow just as appealing in her clothing as out of it. He should say something. Tell her everything would be all right. Yet he had no knowledge of that fact. He just prayed that Cabot's pretty smile would be enough to soothe her.

"There, pretty flower," Cabot said, his voice a lilting timbre. He grasped her chin and lifted her face to his. "Go to your guest room. I'm sure Ivy is awaiting your call."

Violet blinked up at Cabot, then accepted his kiss with one of hers. His own lips tingled for the touch of that tender caress, but he was far too brutish to warrant such care.

She stared at him now, then nodded and left his room.

Victor cursed, dragging his fingers through his hair. "What the hell am I going to do now?"

Cabot shrugged and picked up Victor's jacket where he'd tossed it on the floor. "You're going to take her again, I imagine."

"Yes," Victor admitted. "Rutting bastard of a Hawk that I am, I suppose I will."

"As will I," Cabot said.

Victor couldn't rouse a lick of jealousy at the notion. Instead he imagined the two golden beauties fucking and groaned aloud. "I admit I can't wait to see that."

Cabot nodded, then stroked his cock, visibly hard through his own trousers. "God, the sight of you pounding into her soft, sweet pussy. I nearly came just from watching."

Victor nodded and sank down in the chair nearest the fireplace. "She was a virgin, Cabot. She was so hot and tight I couldn't stop. I nearly died inside of her."

"A poet for a Hawk, I see," Cabot teased. "Are you ready to dress for dinner?"

Victor waved a hand. "Go see to your other duties, man." He lifted his chin at Cabot's erection. "What are you going to do about that?"

"You don't want to suck me?" Cabot asked.

Inexplicably, Victor's mouth watered at the thought having a taste of him. "I've never."

"No matter." He winked. "You will, before this is over. As for this afternoon? Lucky for me, I'm not a Hawk."

"What do you mean?"

"I'll just use my hand and the image of you and Violet to see to myself."

Again Victor was seized with the urge to laugh. Cabot left his room and Victor saw to his own dress. It was all so astounding, this surprise liaison among the three of them. He shouldn't fuck her again. He really shouldn't. Yet the thought of never having her again caused a pain to settle close to the center of his chest.

He'd have to talk with her, of course. When the heat of passion wasn't burning so damned hot he could scarcely breathe. She would want to know where this would leave them once they returned to Ralston House.

They had nearly a fortnight before the holiday, after all. They were stuck here at Hawksfell, the both of them. Cabot was a willing participant, and perhaps Victor's beast would have its fill of fucking before the new year. Then he could go back to being the thoughtful relative and only support for the girl in his care.

He closed his eyes, reveling for the moment in the intense pleasure of coming without the familiar emptiness to follow so swiftly on its heels. He didn't know what the hell all this was but he would enjoy it while he had it.

God knew what would come when this madness was over.

* * * *

Cabot climbed up to his attic room, his balls aching but his heart light. Tasting Violet, bringing her to stunning climax, had surpassed his expectations. But watching Victor take her? He hadn't been lying when he'd said he'd nearly come in his trousers. His big dark body held over her perfect fair form was something he wouldn't forget anytime soon.

He opened his door and stepped inside. As he eased the door closed he worked the top button free of his trousers. He hissed as his fingers brushed over his swollen cock.

"You're not with the baron, Cabot?" Ivy asked from behind him.

His hand stilled and he craned his neck. He saw over his shoulder that, once again, she was stalking him in the hallway.

"I have to ready for dinner service, Ivy." He folded his hands in front of his groin and turned to face her. "Don't you have to see to the countess?"

Ivy nodded. "Yes. I thought I'd take care of Miss Ralston first but her guest room was empty." She tilted her head to one side. "Where do you suppose she could be?"

Cabot felt his cheeks turn pink but he managed a negligent shrug. "How would I know? It's a big house, you know."

"Hmm." Ivy ran her gaze over him. "You look disheveled, Cabot. Much like you did yesterday afternoon."

"What are you implying?"

She let out a gasp. "I know who you've been with!" she said, her eyes narrowed.

Cold fear clutched at his belly. "What?"

"Tillie," she said. "That little kitchen mouse. You're fucking her!"

Cabot nearly laughed at the ridiculous notion. Tillie was not only very young, but as naïve as a child. He'd no sooner fuck her than he would Mrs. Holmes.

"I've not taken Tillie and you'd be wise not to spread such a vile tale, Ivy. The countess doesn't care for gossip, and Mrs. Holmes will recommend she sack you if she gets wind of it."

Ivy paled. "That's true."

"Now stop hounding me and go play with one of the groomsman. What about the new chauffeur? Maybe he'll give you a ride, so to speak."

Ivy clicked her tongue. "Do you think I'm a doxy, Cabot? I don't just want a tumble. Goodness knows I could get one anywhere I wanted." She eyed him again. "Nearly anywhere, that is."

"As I said, I have to ready for dinner service. Go down to the servants' hall. Go down to the carriage house. Go down to the bloody kitchen and help Mrs. Padmont with the bloody stew. I don't care. Just get out of my bloody room!"

Ivy pulled back, then an expression of resignation settled on her face. "Fine, then." She sniffed and lifted her chin. "I know when I'm not wanted."

"Do you?"

Apparently she chose to ignore his meaning. "You can't deny that your shaft is hard for someone, Cabot."

It's hard for two people, actually. He forced himself to keep Victor and Violet's names behind his teeth. "Go, Ivy," he said, more gently this time. "My business is my own."

"Take care," she said in parting.

She left and he prayed that was finally the end of it. He closed the door tight. His exchange with her had taken care of his erection. That was certain. Putting the maid out of his mind, he dressed for dinner service and hurried down to the servants hall.

She'd told him in parting to take care. He would have to do that for sure. Playing with Victor was one thing. He was a Hawk and used to taking his pleasure wherever he might. As for Violet? She was previously a virgin. A passion-starved, eager former virgin, but an innocent nonetheless. She was most definitely in love with Victor, though. Cabot would have to be blind not to see that from the first. Having the both of them as lovers was something he never should attempt. They were both so far above him it would be ridiculous if he didn't know in his soul that they wanted him as much as he did them.

What this would mean after Christmas was anyone's guess. He would simply enjoy himself and keep his heart out of it. He might be sensitive, but he was no simpering fool. Play was play. Two weeks wasn't long enough for his heart to crave more than passion with them. He was sure of it.

* * * *

Violet sat before the small vanity in her guest room, her heart finally beginning to slow. She was clad in only her chemise again, a fresh one this time, and the mirror showed her what a mess she looked. Her hair was tangled and her lips swollen. She was so fair she could see the faint marks left by first Cabot and then Victor's attention to her aching breasts. What had she done?

First, to take a flirtation with Cabot to such lengths, and then to give herself to Victor? She laughed without humor. Truth be told, she hadn't given him anything. She'd taken. Everything he'd had to give. His big body, heavy and wonderful on hers. His thick cock, finally as deep inside of her as she could manage. And yet...

And yet she still craved to make love with Cabot. What was wrong with her?

A knock came at her door then and she dashed her hands over her flaming cheeks. "Come," she called.

Ivy, Lady Hawksfell's maid and on loan for her care, entered. "Good evening, miss."

"Hello, Ivy," Violet answered.

As Ivy set about seeing to Violet's dress and items on the top of the vanity, Violet couldn't help but watch her. She was a very pretty girl, with auburn hair and deep brown eyes. Again she was reminded of Victor's liaisons with the staff of Ralston. He surely would have taken this girl if Violet hadn't been the one to have him today. And what of Cabot? Had he already been with Ivy?

"How long have you worked here, Ivy?" she asked.

"Just over a month, miss." Ivy worked with her hair, ridding it of most of its tangles. "My, your hair is…"

"A mess?" Violet finished for her.

Ivy's hands froze. "Miss, I didn't mean to say anything untoward."

"It is a mess, Ivy. I had a rest and I must have tossed and turned a bit."

By the slant of one of the maid's brows, Violet doubted she swallowed the lie. "A rest?"

Violet couldn't meet her gaze in the mirror so she focused on a spot on the opposite wall. "Yes. I had a walk about the grounds and was fatigued."

Ivy's lips thinned. "The grounds are extensive."

The girl didn't say anything more as she finished with first Violet's hair and then her dress. Her deep purple gown was well suited to the winter's evening in half mourning.

"Thank you for your assistance, Ivy," Violet said as she pulled on her long gloves.

"I'm happy to do it, miss."

As Ivy reached the door she glanced at Violet over her shoulder. "You took a rest. This afternoon?"

Violet's cheeks heated but she nodded. "As I've said."

Ivy smiled. "Forgive me, miss. I would have assisted you out of your dress had you rung for me."

"Thank you, but there was no need, Ivy."

The maid bobbed a curtsey and left at last. Was the girl trying to guess what Violet had been about today? Did she somehow know?

Putting the inquisitive maid out of her mind, she took one last look in the mirror. She was presentable, and looked for all the world like a welcome guest of the Earl of Hawksfell.

It was a pity she would have to face both Victor and Cabot at dinner tonight.

Chapter 8

"Cabot is going to have you tonight, Violet."

Victor's words sent a shaft of desire through Violet's body. Her eyes went to Cabot and her breath caught as he locked the door to Victor's room.

Victor stood behind her, his hands slowly working the buttons of her dress loose. "Cabot tonight, Victor?"

Cabot laughed and turned from the door. His eyes were sparkling in that teasing way she'd come in such a short time to relish.

"It was hell serving at table last night," he said. "Being so close to the two people I can't stop wanting."

Victor cupped her breasts as her corset slipped down. "I want you both, as well." His voice was rough and her body trembled.

Victor shifted and Cabot stepped behind her, his hands in her hair. Pins scattered as he loosened the elaborate coif Ivy had given her.

"You have incredible hair," Cabot said, his fingers stroking through the mass.

It was freeing and a bit wanton, the sensation of a man's fingers caressing her so. She closed her eyes and leaned back. She could feel Victor's lips on her neck as Cabot's fingers continued to work their magic.

"You know, Ivy mentioned the state of your incredible hair when she'd helped you dress last night," Cabot said.

Violet held her breath. What had the girl said to Cabot?

"How did you deflect that particular line of conversation?" Victor asked.

Cabot nuzzled the other side of her neck and she leaned back against him for support. "I said nothing to draw more conversation, believe me."

"Have you—?" Victor bit back whatever he was going to ask but she knew precisely what he meant.

A chill danced over her skin and she straightened. "You and Ivy, Cabot?"

"What? No!" he answered.

She turned, her hands going to his shoulders. "Forgive me, Cabot! I have nerves of steel to presume you were only mine when I am clearly giving myself to both you and Victor."

They both stared at her and the words she'd spoken struck her. She was indeed giving herself to them and taking everything they had to offer. Her cheeks heated and it wasn't a reaction to staring into their handsome faces.

"Oh, I didn't mean..." She couldn't form an excuse for what she'd said. Her throat was thick as she realized she was putting too much of a demand on their broad shoulders.

"I'm not only yours, Violet," Cabot said.

She knew that. Lord, she knew that very well. But to hear him say the words cut her in a way they definitely shouldn't. "I know," she said on a whisper. "You're so pretty and there are so many lovely maids working here."

They glanced at each other, then Cabot smiled brightly. "I didn't mean any other maids."

Her heart began to beat. "Then, who..." When Victor's dark eyes heated, she knew. Cabot meant he was Victor's!

"You and Victor?" she asked dumbly. "Victor, you and Cabot?"

Victor nodded. "Cabot and I."

Images crashed through her mind, blurry and heated. How would the two men be together? "I don't care about the particulars," she breathed. "I can't wait to see the both of you together."

Cabot laughed again and there was a definite curve to Victor's lips.

"My, my," Victor said. "Come here, Violet."

Her body leaned toward the two of them and Victor took her mouth in a searing kiss. His taste was stronger than she remembered, and her mouth watered for more of him. As Victor kissed her, Cabot worked the rest of her clothes free. She felt a slight chill, then her body heated from the fire and their hands on her skin.

Victor picked her up and brought her over to the bed. She was naked now, reclining on the fine bed as she had been just yesterday. Desperately, she needed them to be as naked as she.

"Do take off your clothes," she said, coming up on her elbows.

Cabot chuckled and Victor shrugged. "Should I have my valet strip me, Violet?"

Her breath caught. "Teasing again, Victor?"

He smiled, a larger expression this time. "I suppose I am."

Cabot grabbed Victor's shoulders and worked his jacket free. Facing him, he kissed him as she watched. Her pussy was dripping wet now, her body clenching.

"Oh, you're kissing." She swallowed thickly. "Take off your clothes, please."

They parted and each stripped. They were differently built, as she'd noted yesterday. Today however, with both of them naked, she could appreciate the differences and similarities. Cabot was sculpted and gorgeous, muscular yet lean. Victor was burly, more heavily muscled and powerful. How could she want them both? As they joined her on the bed she put the question out of her mind. She did. Plain and simply put, she wanted them both.

"I'll have a taste of you tonight," Victor rasped, flicking his tongue over one nipple.

She jumped, then arched into his mouth. He bit down briefly, sending a shaft of pleasure straight to her pussy. "Oh, Victor!"

He released her nipple and gave it a long lick. "God, you're delicious." He kissed his way down over her belly and spread her thighs wide. "Mmm, I can't wait to taste your pussy."

His mouth covered her flesh and she bucked. In an instant Cabot was with her, kissing her deeply as he teased the breast Victor had left damp and wanting. His fingers were very skilled, his thumb grazing her nipple as Victor began to suck at her little nub of pleasure. She ran her fingers through Cabot's silky blond hair as he lifted his head. His eyes were dark now, mirroring her desire.

"Do you like what Victor's doing?" he asked.

"Y–yes," she answered, nodding. "What both of you are doing, actually."

"Good." Cabot kissed her lips again, then shifted to take her other breast into his mouth.

She squeezed her eyes shut as sensations overwhelmed her. Victor's big, strong fingers moved in and out of her, teasing her on the inside as his tongue scraped over her clit. She clutched at Cabot's head, earning a moan from him as he sucked harder on her aching nipple. Spreading her legs wider, she urged Victor to finish what he'd started.

His fingers were thick, at least two moving deep inside. There was no barrier to his touch now, no proof of virginity to impede his penetration. She began to tremble, lifting and arching off the bed as her orgasm tore through her. She began to scream when Cabot's mouth covered hers again.

"Shh, sweet flower," he said between kisses. "We might be far from the other rooms, but such enthusiasm still might be overheard."

She caught her breath at last and giggled. Her limbs felt light, but she still couldn't rouse the energy to lift them. "Of course," she murmured.

Victor covered her with his big beautiful body as he had yesterday and kissed her as well. He tasted of himself and of her juices, but she couldn't rouse embarrassment. This was a time out of their life. It was an opportunity to learn what she could and put any reservations aside. Besides, she couldn't grow timid when she so wanted to see her two men together.

"That was astounding," he said, pulling back to lick his lips. "You're delectable."

Her cheeks flamed again as he slanted her a concerned look. "Do you think you're ready for Cabot?"

Her pussy, so recently sated, pulsed with its own answer. Ooh, Cabot would take her now. It was quite a good thing that she wasn't thinking too hard about all of this. Otherwise she just might refuse what would surely be an incredible experience.

"Yes." She turned to Cabot. "Are you ready for me, Cabot?"

He laughed and came to his knees, showing off his impressive erection. "Can you not tell?"

She stared at his cock in the light, finding it as beautiful as the rest of him. Long and thick, straining toward her with a drop of liquid glistening on its head. Seized by a naughty notion, she sat up quickly and stroked her tongue over the tip.

"God!" Cabot cried. "You'll have me coming before I even get inside of you."

She couldn't help but grin. "You've both tasted me. I thought I'd taste you."

Victor growled something under his breath, then knelt on her other side. "Taste me."

She eyed his erection. He seemed even larger than Cabot, if that was possible. There was a drop of cream on his cock's head as well, so she turned and licked him. He hissed out a breath and leaned back on his hands. "Suck me."

She pulled back for a moment at his harsh command, hearing the need in his voice. Then closed her mouth over him. He groaned and held himself still as she began to suckle. Her pussy grew hot and prickly again, her arousal fueled by Victor's reaction. Cabot grabbed her hips and drew her up on her knees. The man knew what he was doing, for she held herself on her hands on either side of Victor's narrow hips and bobbed her head a bit. When he moaned again, she nearly smiled. Then Cabot slipped a hand beneath to stroke her pussy.

Shivering, she spread her thighs to allow him easier access. Oh, she could come again just from this attention!

"I'm going to take you from behind, Violet," Cabot said, his mouth close to her ear. "I didn't think you'd be ready, but you're soaking wet."

His fingers drove inside and she shuddered. From behind, he'd said. Oh, she wanted to know what that felt like!

Lifting her head a fraction from Victor's delicious cock, she sighed. "Please, Cabot."

He shifted and the bed dipped a bit. Leaning close to her, he brought his cock up against her pussy. The friction was delightful and she smiled at him over her shoulder before returning to the task at hand. Victor's cock felt even larger now and she glanced up at him. His head was thrown back and his eyes shut as he reveled in her kisses. His lashes were thick on his cheeks and she never found him more beautiful. Her mouth closed over him again and she took him deep in her throat as Cabot moved to enter her.

"You're so small, Violet," Cabot said on a breath. "Take me. Take all of me."

He eased inside of her and she wriggled her bottom. He gave one cheek a light slap then began to move in and out of her. "This feels so good," he groaned.

"Her mouth, Cabot," Victor gasped. "I'm going to come. So help me, I'm going to come!"

She sucked and licked at him and barely registered his shout of completion as he came in her mouth. His taste was strong, delectable, and she swallowed. The next instant Cabot held on tight to her hips and began to pound into her.

"Cabot!" she cried, trying to hold on as she twisted the sheets beneath in her hands. He worked at an angle and his cock touched on a place inside her that seemed ultrasensitive. "That feels... Oh!"

He didn't say anything to her inadequate exclamation. No, he just continued to take her harder and harder as she began to come. Victor must have recovered, for he drew her upward and shifted until she was clutching at his shoulders. When he cupped her breast, pinching one nipple, she climaxed. Cabot didn't cease, just moved in and out of her as Victor held her close. Sobbing, she came again between them. As if from a distance she heard Cabot cry out himself as he spilled deep inside her.

They collapsed on the bed, sweaty and tangled and sated. She couldn't speak for them but she was exhausted. Her body still tingled and quivered, and she burrowed down into the soft coverlet. "I shall never forget this."

* * * *

Cabot froze beside her. Her words brought reality crashing through his pleasure soaked brain. This time had a set end. He knew that. They weren't meant for him. He caught Victor's gaze, but saw nothing clear there. That was no surprise. The man wore a mask thicker than any other Hawk he'd ever seen.

"We have until Christmas," was all Victor said.

Cabot nodded, taking the words at face value. He brought his lips to Violet's flushed cheek and kissed her. "We'll make it even more memorable, Violet."

She murmured something, not opening her eyes as she sighed. Memorable. Memories were all he would have left after they returned to Ralston. Ah, but what memories they were. Victor's cock, deep in Violet's mouth as his burly body arched sharply. Violet's pert ass tight against his belly as he fucked her, urging two orgasms out of her before losing his own control.

"You sucked Victor's cock," he observed. "I admit, I've longed to do that."

To his satisfaction, she opened her eyes at that. Interest filled their deep blue depths. "What? You would…" She licked her lips. "Oh, is that how you make love?"

Victor's cheeks turned a bit ruddy and Cabot longed to tease him a bit as well. He stifled the urge, knowing the man wasn't as comfortable with banter as he was himself. "Not yet, no. Victor took me."

Her mouth fell open. "How?"

He smiled and brushed the hair off his brow. Leveling her a look, he waited for her to grasp the possibility. A light came into her eyes and she arched a brow. "Victor *took* you. In your bottom?"

Cabot nodded.

"I fucked him, Violet," Victor said. "Like I fucked you."

Cabot heard a thread of regret in his voice. A shade of trepidation. His gorgeous dark Hawk eyes were clouded and Cabot gave into the urge to reach across Violet's slight form to grasp his shoulder in comfort. "He's a magnificent lover, isn't he?"

He directed his words to Violet but caught Victor's gaze. Heat simmered between them, enhanced now that they'd both had her. He'd never shared a woman. He'd never shared a man either, but these two made him throw all previous notions out the large leaded windows. He began to simmer, his cock stirring at the notion of having them both again.

"I'm a greedy fellow," he said to Violet. He faced her now. "I want you both and I want to give myself to you both."

She bit her lip, then nodded. "Then I'm greedy as well." She came up on her knees, brushing her glorious hair back over her shoulders. "Victor, what say you?"

"About?" Victor asked.

She smiled, a bright expression he hadn't seen on her face before. "Should we both take Cabot?"

Cabot caught his breath as Victor slowly smiled.

Chapter 9

Two days passed before they could make good on Violet's promise. Cabot's body hummed almost nonstop, his balls aching for what he could only guess would be incredible release. Just climbing the stairs to Victor's guest chamber caused a combination of pain and postponed pleasure to radiate through his body. They were both going to take him? God, just the thought of how they might go about it was enough to make him stroke himself to release the past two nights.

He entered the room and shut the door tight. "Now I know what you Hawks go through."

Victor arched a dark brow and turned from the mirror. "Do you? How so?"

Cabot shrugged and took Victor's jacket from him. "The constant need, Victor. My balls are aching and my cock twitches at the least provocation."

"Provocation?" What he now knew passed for a smile crossed Victor's face. "Not the little maid Ivy, I hope."

"God, no. She's a pretty thing but nothing compared to our girl."

Victor lifted his chin as Cabot loosened his tie. "Our girl."

"Violet is everything." Cabot took a breath and pressed forward. "I know you've known her forever and it's only been a few days since I first glimpsed her beautiful face, but I'm falling."

Victor grabbed his wrist, his hold firm. "Falling?" His eyes were rounded with what he could only guess was surprise. "You love Violet?"

Cabot pulled gently out of his grasp. "Love? I don't know about that. I admit I've never felt anything like this before the two of you."

Victor's eyes sharpened. "The two of us?"

Cabot held up his hands. "I'm not staking claim, Victor. Not on Violet and certainly not on you."

Something like a shadow crossed Victor's face. "Certainly not me. Because I'm a Hawk."

Cabot wished he could stop this conversation but something compelled him to continue. "You are a Hawk. A bloody baron, Victor. And Violet, though a goddess I cannot resist, is far above me as well."

To his astonishment, Victor grabbed his shoulders and pulled him close. He couldn't look away from those dark eyes. "I want you, Cabot. Like I've never wanted another man. Hell, I didn't think I could want someone as much as I desire Violet, but there it is."

Cabot attempted to say something, anything, but Victor crushed his mouth to his. His tongue dove into his mouth and Cabot felt his body react fully now. He felt Victor's cock hard against his and pressed closer still. His heart raced as Victor's hands cupped his ass. This was bliss, being held by this man. The only thing missing was Violet.

"Ooh, that's just lovely!" Violet said from the doorway.

Victor lifted his head and threw Violet another of his small smiles. "Shut the door, Violet."

Cabot followed the direction of his gaze and saw their girl gaping at them with her eyes darkened to purple. She blinked, then jumped to do as he bade. She drifted closer, her hands clasped in front of her remarkable bosom.

"The two of you are so beautiful together." She tugged at her bodice. "I want to see you stripped again and loving each other."

Cabot nearly came in his trousers. "What of your promise, Violet?"

Surprisingly, she giggled. "Oh, we're going to take you Cabot. Mmm, I can scarcely wait."

After another crushing kiss, Victor stepped back and tore at his clothes. "I daresay I don't need my valet to see to this."

"Your valet is otherwise engaged," Cabot answered, removing his livery and stripping down to the skin. He turned and worked on Violet's dress. "I can smell you, Violet. Sweet and hot, little flower."

She giggled again and wriggled until her dress and underpinnings fell to the floor. Cabot stepped back, staring at her gorgeous curves. Her breasts rose and fell with her every breath, her nipples pebbled and tempting. Bending his head, he took one in his mouth. She gasped and clutched at his head.

"Not far, Cabot!" She purred and pressed closer. "We're supposed to take you."

In answer he fell to his knees and buried his face in her pussy. "Your cunt smells so good." He used his thumbs to spread her to his tongue and licked her. "Mmm."

Victor stepped behind her and cupped her breasts. "Should we give our girl a ride before?"

Cabot glanced up to see dark intent stamped on Victor's face. He shook his head and stood, rubbing his bare chest over her tight pink nipples. She stared up at him and he smiled. "I want her wet for us, I think. Hungry."

She moaned, letting out a sigh when Victor bent his head and nibbled the side of her neck.

"Soaking wet and ready," Victor said. He released her and came to stand behind Cabot. "What of you, Cabot? Are you ready?"

His cock began to pound as Victor brought his shaft up against his ass. With Victor at his back and Violet at his front, he reasoned he might just lose his mind before his seed. Violet's delicate hands trailed over the front of him, teasing his nipples and stroking his belly. Victor's large hands grabbed his thighs and pressed closer. He bit Cabot's ear as he'd teased Violet's. "Cream, Violet."

Those words caused Cabot's body to flush hot. "In the top drawer, love."

Violet hurried to the dressing table and found the jar. "Victor, you'll use this to..." She grinned. "Oh, I don't think I'll be needing this."

Victor actually barked out a laugh as he took the jar from her. "Let's give Cabot what we promised."

"And soon, please!" Cabot moaned. "I'm going to come on the carpet otherwise."

Victor didn't waste any more time. He used the cream to slide two fingers into Cabot's ass and it was nearly perfect. He wanted more, though. He needed Victor's big cock deep inside as he held Violet close again. "Come here, Violet."

She stood in front of him again, all flushed and pink. Victor leaned forward and took her mouth then, and the sounds they both made caused Cabot's balls to ache. She twined her fingers in Cabot's hair and kissed him then, and he could taste Victor on her tongue. With the man behind him, teasing his hole with his cock, and Violet renewing her caresses he just closed his eyes and surrendered.

Victor wrapped an arm around Cabot's chest and sank into him. Groaning, Cabot reached up to grab onto his neck as Victor began to thrust. Slowly, inch by inch, Cabot took him. Violet began to kiss his chest, her hand grasping his erection. He was being turned inside out, every nerve humming as he sank against Victor's broad chest. It was like heaven.

"You're tight, Cabot," Victor growled in his ear. "Are you eager to come?"

Cabot moaned an answer in the positive.

"Suck him, Violet," Victor said.

Cabot shuddered at his words. "God, yes."

Victor surged forward as Violet's full lips closed over the head of his cock. She sucked as he moved with Victor's motions, going deep down her throat as Victor increased his thrusts. His every nerve was stretched taut and he couldn't hold on any longer. His orgasm crashed through his body, wringing him dry as he came in hot spurts down her throat. Victor's fingers bit into his hips as he came as well, sounds of bliss coming from him as he held onto Cabot.

"Oh, take me!" Violet cried.

Cabot tried to catch his breath as he opened his eyes. She was kneeling on the floor, her hands on her beautiful breasts.

Victor withdrew and swore softly. "Watching her suck you, Cabot. I couldn't hold on."

Cabot nodded, leaning back to take a kiss from Victor. "What of our girl?"

Victor's smile widened a fraction. "Take her. Lick her. Make her come."

She came shakily to her feet and grabbed Cabot's shoulders. "Oh, lick me!"

He grabbed her and shifted, tumbling her back to the floor. He buried his face in her cunt, lapping at the juices that drenched her. "You're close, aren't you?" he said between licks.

She arched sharply. "Lick my pussy, Cabot!"

He drove his fingers deep in her pussy, teasing upward as she bucked. Her clit was hidden by her swollen lips so he spread her with his thumbs as he had earlier. Driving his tongue inside her cunt, he fucked her with his mouth.

She was trembling now, her head thrashing on the carpet as she tugged madly on his hair. "Yes, yes, yes!"

Her taste brought his cock back to life. He had to get inside of her. As she began to come, he pulled away. Her eyes snapped open, glaring up at him. "Don't stop!"

In one smooth motion he impaled her. She screamed as she came around him, her legs still spread wide as she scored his back with her nails. His second orgasm of the night tore through him and he climaxed inside of her.

The combined release first Victor then she gave him caused him to nearly black out. He somehow managed to hold himself up on his arms as he sucked in a breath. His heart hammered in his chest and it was several moments before he could rouse himself.

"I may simply die right here," he rasped.

Victor laughed again, the sound rusty, and he settled on the bed. "If I wasn't exhausted, I'd join you."

Violet murmured sweet sounds beneath him and let her arms fall back on the floor above her head. He kissed her sweet lips and let his worries slip away.

He just felt too damned good to think about what the future would bring.

* * * *

Victor stood at the back of the manor, the chill of the frozen ground seeping through the soles of his hunting boots. He'd spent the morning with Gabriel and Matthew Hawk, the earl's half brother, but couldn't seem to focus on the partridge. He'd made some sort of excuse to leave the other Hawks. Gabriel seemed to take him at his word, but Matthew eyed him far too closely. Victor hadn't spent much time with him, but knew he lived in the dower house very close to the manor. He must know more of the goings on than even the earl, if what Victor had gleaned was true.

Matthew was married to a former parlor maid, a lovely young woman Victor had met at dinner two nights past. There were whispers of another in the marriage, a William both Matthew and his wife Posy spoke of often and with much affection. He didn't believe it could be the stoic first footman William, though. Victor wanted to ask Cabot if this could true, but gossip was never something he relished. A thought occurred to him then. Was gossip circulating through the manor about him and Cabot? Or worse, the two of them and Violet? Perhaps he should put a stop to it all. The mere thought of giving them up caused a clenching in his heart.

Their last time together, three nights past, had been incredible. He and Violet had loved Cabot until the man came apart between them. His own orgasm had stunned him speechless. He could only watch as

Cabot licked Violet and then, remarkably, fucked her so hard Victor nearly felt it. Shoving his hands deep into his pockets, he began to stroll.

His mind worked on what Cabot had said the previous time they'd been together. The finality in his tone as he promised Violet to make their liaison memorable. Cabot didn't need to make an effort as far as Victor was concerned. He would never forget this time. The fact that days had passed without a liaison fueled his need, but not in the usual manner. Yes, his beast was always lurking. Eager for a ride, as it were. Yet this time it felt decidedly different. His cock wanted release but only with Cabot or Violet.

He'd never known his lusts to crave anyone specific. He'd recently spent time around several very good-looking people here at Hawksfell Manor yet there had been no stirring whatsoever. Maids and footman and gorgeous ladies did nothing for his cock or his mind. It was astounding. Only a glance from Violet or a glimpse of Cabot made him rock hard.

The length of their visit at the manor was nearly over now, or it certainly felt that way. He couldn't bear the thought of leaving Cabot behind when he and Violet returned to Ralston. He still hadn't talked to her about all of this, either. He'd managed to avoid being alone with her outside of his guest bedroom, coward that he was. They certainly haven't discussed what their relationship would be when they took up their previous situation at home. Not that he relished a return to that stilted intercourse while he fucked every servant under his roof. There was the matter of Cabot as well.

Violet was obviously falling for Cabot as much as the man was for her. Their coupling that last night had been a remarkable thing to see but not because they were both so bloody beautiful. It was the kiss they'd shared after the storm ebbed. It had been tender and so sweet he could almost taste it.

He could arrange it so that those two stayed together. He didn't quite know how but maybe, with his damned Hawk money, he could set them up to have the life he had no hope for himself. Maybe in a pretty little house not far from Ralston. Despite his own flawed nature he knew he wouldn't be able to bear it if they were far from him. He would keep his distance, of course. It might kill him but he would stay away from the both of them. They were good, sweet people who deserved happiness.

Happiness wasn't his due. That was certain. As a Hawk he'd never deserved that. His curse was a part of him, and he wouldn't have them at Ralston while he continued to fuck the staff and ache for release even they couldn't give him. He certainly wouldn't marry, as the earl and his brother had. It wasn't meant for him. Hawks simply didn't do forever, despite the evidence to the contrary here at Hawksfell Manor.

He wasn't aware he was crying until the tears turned to ice on his cheeks.

Chapter 10

Violet scrutinized her dress in the glass. It was a pretty shade of purple but she was growing tired of even this half mourning. A stab of guilt struck her. "I'm sorry, Aunt Jane."

Shaking her head, she picked up her gloves and pulled them on. Ivy was quiet behind her, smoothing the last of the wrinkles out of her dress and brushing off her shoulders.

"Miss, you look lovely," the maid said.

There was something in her tone, a wistfulness Violet had heard often enough in her own voice. She turned to look at Ivy. "Is something troubling you, Ivy?"

The maid started to shake her head, then gave a quick nod. "Forgive me, miss. I've been out of sorts with the holiday coming and all."

"Do you have no family then?"

"None of import," Ivy answered. "Oh, my grandmother is still alive, but she is in London and I'm here in Yorkshire. There is no one else close to me." Her pretty brown eyes went wide. "Oh, don't think I'm not grateful for my position! To become a lady's maid in as fine a house as Hawksfell is amazing for a girl like me."

Violet felt a kinship for this girl despite their difference in status. Violet had no family but Victor, and that relationship had crossed far over from familial. She turned to face the maid fully.

"I imagine you like working for Lady Hawksfell, though?"

"I do. She's lovely and kind and not demanding in the least." Ivy smiled and waved her hand over Violet's dress and hair. "As you see."

"Yes, I've found all the Hawks to be very accommodating."

Violet's own statement struck her as odd though, considering just how accommodating Victor had been to her and Cabot during their stay here. So many times she'd loved them both, nearly losing her mind with the pleasure of it. She laughed, a choked sound that brought tears to her eyes.

"Miss?" Ivy touched Violet's wrist, the gesture gentle. "Are you all right?"

Violet reined her in her emotions with a thread breath. "It must be the holiday. Just two weeks ago I never expected to spend it with family, let alone so many of Vic... of Lord Ralston's."

"Lord Ralston is your cousin," Ivy said.

"Third cousin," Violet corrected with another laugh. "That seems significant."

"You care about him," Ivy said softly.

Violet gave a slow nod. "I do."

Ivy blinked. "I'd thought that you and..." She waved a hand. "Forgive me, miss. I believed someone else held your heart."

Violet swallowed. "Someone else does indeed hold my heart."

Ivy's mouth dropped open. "Like the countess."

It was a bald statement and Violet knew in that moment the lady's maid would know the intimate details of her employer. Lady Hawksfell loved both the earl and Michael Crowley. Her legs going weak, Violet slumped into the chair before the vanity.

"The earl loves both of them?" Violet whispered.

Ivy nodded, her cheeks bright red. "I shouldn't have spoken of it, miss." She turned and busied herself with the hairpins on the vanity's smooth surface. "I suspected he had found someone else."

Violet's heard pounded. She had to ask. She simply had to ask. "Who are you talking about, Ivy?"

"Cabot," Ivy breathed. She faced Violet again. "Cabot fell in love with someone else."

Ivy was so pretty to Violet. She'd suspected Victor would have wanted to take her but now she believed Cabot had already been with her.

"Were you involved with Cabot?"

"No. Never." Ivy shrugged. "He is just so pretty, miss. He flirts and teases all the maids, but when I did so in return he went all cold on me."

Violet felt a smile spread over her face and bit her lip to contain it. This shouldn't matter. She herself had no hold over Cabot or even Victor for that matter. Yet she couldn't bear it if Cabot had done to this girl all the delicious things he'd done to her. Lord, she might be selfish but she didn't want Victor or Cabot loving anyone but her and each other.

"It's all right," Ivy said with a smile of her own. "Cabot found love with someone else, I suppose. There's no other answer."

Relief flooded Violet. If a well-connected personal maid in a big house full of gossip like Ivy didn't know about Cabot's recent liaisons Violet could be fairly certain no one else did. She took the maid's hand in hers. "Did you love Cabot, then?"

"No," Ivy admitted. "He's just so very pretty."

"He is," was all Violet would admit now.

Ivy seemed to remember her situation in the next instant. "Please don't tell the countess I was passing tales, miss!"

"I would never do that," Violet assured her.

Ivy's slender shoulders slumped with obvious relief. "Thank you, miss. I'll be back this evening to help you undress."

"There will be no need for that."

Ivy looked at her in question. Well, Violet couldn't tell her that in all likelihood she wouldn't return to her own guest room until well past midnight. She planned to ring in the holiday with her two men.

"It's Christmas Eve, Ivy. Please don't trouble yourself with my care tonight."

Ivy nodded and left the room at last. Over the past few days, as the end of their visit loomed larger, the three of them hadn't had much chance to relive the sensual magic they'd shared. Oh, there was the one time in one of the empty rooms in the bachelor's wing the other day.

She'd sucked Cabot's beautiful cock deep down her throat as Victor had fucked her like mad from behind. It had been too short an encounter in her opinion, despite the incredible explosion of pleasure she'd experienced. She wanted more than that now. She wanted the tender cuddling the three of them had indulged in a few times before. Their bodies snug against hers, stroking and teasing and comforting. She'd longed for affection as well as passion, and for a brief time she'd believed she'd found it. Victor had held her heart for so long and now Cabot was firmly ensconced there as well. He teased her and made her laugh. Incredibly, he made Victor more at ease as well.

It would end and soon, however. This time out of her life would cease and she would once more have nothing. Well, a bit more than nothing. Memories. Sweet, hot memories that made her melt to recall. She glanced in the mirror again and lifted her chin.

"I'll have Victor's kinship and a fine home," she told her reflection. No tender connection to Victor. No Cabot at all. But tonight? It was Christmas Eve and she was going to get the gift she really wanted.

One last time with her two men.

* * * *

The manor was lit with electric lights and many candles. The scent of cinnamon and mulled wine and plum pudding filled the dining room. The table was set with every conceivable holiday delight and crammed full of Hawks and their wives and partners. Cabot moved about with precision as the earl and his family sat themselves and began their feast.

Victor and Violet were turned out beautifully. Dressed formally, Victor was a dark delectable specimen. The gorgeous Violet was clad in a gown the color of her eyes and the many lights and candles caught the gold in her hair. His mouth watered for a taste of her full lips and his body longed for the clasp of Victor's strong arms.

Dragging his gaze from them, he fought to focus on his job.

"William is joining us full-time at the dower house!" Posy said with a laugh. "Isn't that true, Matthew?"

Matthew Hawk slid a glance at his wife and smiled. "An inopportune moment to make such an announcement, but it is indeed true."

"Carstairs will lose his sour expression over William's absence for Christmas Eve then," the earl put in.

Lady Hawksfell laughed. "Carstairs can be prickly, but he sees to the running of your house, Gabriel."

Michael Crowley said something in answer but Cabot didn't catch it. Instead he ran the possibilities through his mind as he refilled wine glasses. William was at last taking up with Matthew and Posy. That left the position of first footman vacant. Cabot knew he was the man next in line for that position. It was what he'd longed for and what he deserved for his faithful service. And yet...

"William the first footman?" Violet asked.

Conversation stilled for a heartbeat, then they all began to chatter.

"Former first footman," Patrick Hawk said. "More staffing issues for Thomas, I imagine."

The earl's man-of-business, Thomas Grantley, shook his head. "I shouldn't be surprised."

"Why is that, pray tell?" Derek Hawk asked with a wink. "Diana, why should that be?"

Derek's wife Diana, a woman nearly as lovely as Violet, just shook her head with a smile. "If the earl has trouble keeping his staff, we shouldn't tease him, Derek."

"If the earl didn't have so many relatives perhaps this wouldn't be an issue," Michael Crowley laughed.

Cabot hid his own smile. It was true that every time a Hawk came to stay at the manor one member or another of Hawksfell staff came to find new positions. Usually as wives or partners, if what he'd observed over the past few months could be believed. The lucky

William was a prime example of such circumstances.

"Grantley will see that we are amply served, Millicent," the earl said.

The table murmured their agreement while Mr. Grantley reddened. Cabot backed out of the room before Victor could catch his eye. It was enough being in the room with the both of them. He wouldn't want either to believe he expected such fortune in his own life. Not love or a permanent pairing with a Hawk and his lovely partner. If he was promoted to first footman he would be grateful for the position and go on with his life as planned.

"Another year, Cabot," Mr. Carstairs said as he entered the butler's pantry. "Happy Christmas."

Cabot smiled at the butler. "Happy Christmas, Mr. Carstairs."

"Very different from last year's celebration, isn't it?"

Cabot simply nodded. Last year there were none but the previous earl and his son, and there was no celebrating that Cabot saw. No, the late earl was a rutting bastard with none of Gabriel Hawk's care or consideration. He supposed the fact that Mrs. Holmes all but raised him was the cause for their differences despite their shared lusts.

Mr. Carstairs cleared his throat. "I suppose you overheard that bit about William."

"Yes."

"It seems you'll be elevated to his position."

"I'd be honored."

The butler appeared pleased by Cabot's response. "Very good. Go see how the lower footmen are serving. Holiday or no, we have our duties."

Cabot said nothing more as he left the pantry. All seemed to be going well in the dining room and would no doubt continue into the parlor as the Hawks continued their celebration. After taking another lingering look at Victor and Violet, he went downstairs to the servants' hall.

He couldn't guess how late Victor would keep to the festivities but he was eager to have him and Violet again. It seemed like far too long since he'd held them both. Their last encounter had been incredible, a quick meeting in the bachelor's wing that swiftly led to Violet sucking him as Victor fucked her nice and hard from behind. They'd all come together, in sync in passion.

"Lord Ralston called for you," Mrs. Holmes said as he settled down at the table in the common room.

He managed to keep his features even as he looked up at the housekeeper. "So early?"

"He didn't seem to be enjoying the festivities once dinner was concluded." She smiled. "So many Hawks can be a bit much for a man used to solitude."

Cabot reasoned she was right on that score. Mrs. Holmes was shrewd and no one cared for the earl and his relatives more than she. Victor had seemed quite isolated tonight, even in a room crowded with his relatives and Violet.

Tamping down the hum of lust zinging through his body, he rose and straightened his livery. "Good night, Mrs. Holmes. And Happy Christmas."

The housekeeper tilted her head to one side, her eyes sharp. "Happy Christmas, Cabot."

There was more the woman wasn't saying but Cabot wasn't going to press her. He'd find himself crying on her shoulder about both Victor and Violet and he couldn't have that. He nodded and left the servants' hall for the stairs at the back of the manor.

As he gained Victor's room, his cock was hard and throbbing. Opening the door, he found Victor stripped and wearing his dressing gown. Thick burgundy draped over his magnificent form and Cabot sucked in a breath.

His dark hair was brushed back from his face and his eyes were intent.

"Victor," was all he could say.

Victor shrugged a broad shoulder. "I thought I could manage to undress myself and give my valet a bit of a present for Christmas."

Cabot grinned. "You're teasing me again."

"I suppose I've learned from you." Victor's face sobered then he came closer. "Get naked, Cabot. Our girl will be here soon."

Cabot didn't need to be asked twice. He was soon stripped naked, his body aching for release.

Victor eyed his cock and smiled. "Violet will love a ride on that, I wager."

"What of yours?" Cabot asked, untying Victor's belt. He stared down at his magnificent length. "Won't our girl want a taste of you?"

They were close and Cabot could smell him. Could feel his heat. "I'm going to fuck her ass while you take her."

Cabot nearly came at the prospect. "Do you believe she'll want that?"

"Both of us inside of her? I know she's hot and takes everything we give her."

Cabot agreed. "Perhaps you shouldn't put it to her quite that way."

"Oh?" Victor's smile was tight. "How should we tell her?"

"Tell me what?" Violet asked.

Cabot turned and watched as her eyes ran greedily over him and Victor. "There you are, love."

She stepped into the room and reached up to wrap her arms around his neck. "Tell me what?" she asked again, bringing her lips to his.

Cabot kissed her sweet mouth and pulled back. "Victor and I are both going to love you."

"But you have already." She blinked, her eyes going to Victor. "Haven't you?"

Victor stepped close and stroked her cheek. "Not like tonight."

She trembled at his words and Cabot suddenly couldn't wait to get her between them. It would be one hell of a Christmas gift and a wonderful way to say good-bye.

Chapter 11

Violet felt the heat of them both through her far too many layers of clothing. Her nipples tightened in her corset and her pussy throbbed. "Get me out of this dress, please."

Victor stepped away and let Cabot see to the matter. Cabot was quite skilled with his hands, his fingers teasing and tickling, and she was soon as naked as they were. Victor cupped one of her breasts from behind as Cabot bent down to lick the nipple. She gasped and let her head rest against Victor's chest. Their scents combined to make her weak with wanting and she clutched at Cabot's shoulders. He began to suckle her and she gasped.

"Do you doubt my assertions now, Cabot?" Victor asked, his body rigid behind her.

"What assertions?" she asked, forcing her eyes open again.

Cabot lifted his head and grinned at Victor over her shoulder. "Not a bit."

His fingers stroked over her, spreading her pussy and delving inside. Letting her legs fall open, she leaned into Victor again. Victor cock pressed between her cheeks as Cabot's teased her hip. Cabot's mouth returned to her aching breast and he gently teethed her. She was soaking wet now. Cabot's fingers tormented her pussy as Victor held her upright. His hands were busy as well, stroking and teasing her bottom. Then he eased one finger into her hole and she shivered. His finger was slick and smooth inside of her.

"Victor?" she asked, trying to make sense of what they were doing.

"Cream, Violet. I'm getting you ready," he answered, his breath hot on her neck. "I'm going to fuck your pretty little ass while Cabot's in your pussy."

His words were compelling. "Oh, is that possible?" she asked.

In answer, Victor moved two fingers inside of her as Cabot's withdrew. They each reversed their motion and began a rhythm that soon had her panting. She could well imagine their cocks buried inside of her and ached for it. Their bodies hot against her front and back, their cocks giving her all she could take. She nearly climaxed right then.

"I need to come," she whimpered. "Please..."

Victor didn't cease his movements as Cabot dropped to his knees before her. His fingers continued to thrust as he sucked on her clit. She was keening now, her voice strange to her ears as she surrendered to their ministrations. Cabot's tongue was wild on her as they both drove her over the edge. She nearly fainted in their grasp as her orgasm shot through her, sharp and wild.

"I have to fuck you," Victor said, taking his fingers from her. "Cabot, take her on the bed."

Cabot stood and kissed her as she slowly opened her eyes. "Are you ready for a ride you'll never forget?"

She grinned like a fool. "Happy Christmas to me."

Cabot laughed and even Victor smiled as they managed to get her on the bed. It was a good thing they assisted her, as her legs were so weak she could scarcely walk. Cabot began to kiss and caress her again as he placed her on his lap. She was straddling his hard thighs, his cock just at her cunt. She was swollen and eager now.

"Get inside me, Cabot," she whispered.

"In a few moments, love," he said.

He began to kiss her and she felt the bed dip as Victor came behind her. It was like before, standing together, but even more of their bodies touched hers now. Victor cupped her bottom and she braced herself. His fingers felt strange and wonderful inside her bottom. What would his very large cock feel like?

"I'll try to go slow," Victor said. "I vow I'll try to go slow."

Cabot caught her chin and brought her face to his. "You trust Victor, don't you?"

She nodded and he kissed her as a reward.

"And me?" he asked.

"I do trust you," she said on a breath.

He smiled and she felt it straight to her heart. "Good."

"I have to get inside you," Victor said, bracing his hands on her hips. "Now."

She felt him at her hole, thick and hot, and her heart skipped. He must have used more of his cream, but the next moment he was there, sinking inch by inch into her as she felt more full than ever before.

"God, you're so tight," Victor bit out. He began to move and she moaned. "Are you all right?"

Her pussy throbbed in answer, greedy for its own due. "Yes, yes," she panted as her heart began to race.

Victor grunted something to that and began to move again. His thrusts were sure and swift and she felt his body so close behind her. Sweat sheened her skin as she moved against him. Her nipples grazed Cabot's chest and she grabbed onto his shoulders.

"I need you, Cabot," she gasped. "Please."

Cabot kissed her throat, her ear. His breath was harsh and she felt his need in his rigid body and straining cock against her belly. "What do you need, Violet?"

"I need you in my pussy," she said, arching back as Victor drove deeper. "Please, Cabot."

Cabot didn't say a word as he shifted beneath her. Positioning his cock at her pussy, he eased her down until he was completely inside of her. It was heaven, the two of them loving her as they had with their fingers. It was so much more, each of their shafts moving in concert as she tried to hold onto her sanity.

"You're inside?" Victor asked. "Move, man. Ah, I can feel you!"

Cabot moaned in answer, increasing his thrusts as he worked her with his cock. "I feel you, Victor," he said, his voice hushed.

Sliding against them, Cabot against her breasts and Victor against her back, was like paradise. She had them and they had her and she wanted this to last forever. Trembling, she could feel her orgasm starting. Drenched with juices, she bowed back and let out a cry as she came hard between them. Neither man ceased, both their cocks moving in rhythm as she felt another climax begin. Her head spun and her body pulsed.

"I'm coming," Cabot said, driving deeper. "Violet, your pussy... Victor!"

"I can't hold on," Victor growled. "Violet, love, I'm going to come!"

Her breath caught. Victor had never called her love before. Then she was lost as another climax overtook her. They shuddered around her, deep inside of her, as they both finally succumbed.

The next thing she knew she was collapsed on Cabot's chest, a sweaty tangle of her hair wrapped around him as Victor withdrew and fell beside them on the bed. Her legs were stretched out on either side of Cabot's body and his cock still pulsed inside her pussy, tugging at her core.

"That was better than I could have imagined," Cabot said. "You're amazing, love."

"Love," she breathed, her eyes squeezed shut.

Something niggled at her. Something Victor had said. Turning, she pushed her hair off her face and raised herself slowly up on her arms. Facing Victor, she opened her eyes to stare deep into his dark ones.

"You called me love," she said.

His brows rose, then his usual coolness settled on his features. "I'm sorry."

"You're sorry?" she asked.

"I can't be what you need," he said.

She gaped at him. She climbed off of Cabot. He moved and now sat, brushing his blond hair off his damp forehead.

"What is this, Victor?" he asked.

Victor grumbled, covering his eyes with one arm. "I can't be what either of you need."

She shared a glance with Cabot, who now looked resigned. "What is going on?" she asked him.

Cabot just shook his head. "I'm not sure, but I don't believe we're going to have a very happy Christmas."

She turned back to Victor. "What do you mean?"

"I'm going to give you up, Violet. Both of you." He swallowed and removed his arm to gaze up at her. "This, I vow."

The pain in his eyes cut her. "You're giving us up?"

"Yes. But I plan to take you both back with me."

"What?" Cabot asked. "As your bloody valet?"

"No!" Victor said.

Violet folded her arms and glared at him. "So you'll take us back with you as what? Pets?"

Victor sat up. "I'll see that you're both settled and can be together."

"Without you?" she asked.

He nodded. "I can't keep myself to you both, Violet. My curse…"

"Is broken," Cabot said, his voice low.

Violet's pulse tripped. "Is that true?"

Hope flared for a moment in Victor's eyes, then he shook his head. "No. I'm not fit for the two of you."

Her eyes pricked with tears and she let them fall. "How can you say that? I love you."

Victor's mouth dropped open. "What?"

"I love you, too," Cabot said.

* * * *

Victor stared at the two beautiful people professing their love and sorely wished he could accept their words. "You can't love me."

"Why the hell not?" Cabot crossed his arms, affecting Violet's posture.

"Violet loves you, Cabot."

She gasped, her hand covering her mouth. Cabot grinned and took that hand in his. "You love me?"

She nodded. "I do. I admit, I never thought I could love two people."

"Me either, but I do," Cabot said.

She stared, then giggled. "You love me?" she asked Cabot.

Cabot nodded and kissed her. "And we both love Victor, apparently."

She nodded and they faced him again. They looked fierce and radiant and Victor would have looked away if he had any strength.

"I'm a Hawk," he muttered.

"Tell me what that has to do with this?" Violet asked. "Did you not see the happiness in front of your face this evening?"

Victor's mind went back to the celebration with the Hawks tonight. There was love there, and connections he couldn't dismiss. "I don't understand it."

"You're not cursed, Victor," Cabot said. "At least not any longer. Have you fucked anyone but us while you were here?"

"No," he had to answer.

"Did you want anyone else?" Violet asked, her voice trembling.

"No," he said again.

"Then tell me what the issue is?" Cabot's brow furrowed. "It's because I'm just a servant, isn't it?"

"God, no!" Victor stabbed his fingers into his hair in frustration. "I don't have any issue with you or your status, Cabot. I…care for you."

"You care for me?" Cabot asked.

"You love him!" Violet said.

He gave a shaky nod. "And you," he admitted to her.

She clutched her hand to her throat. "You love me?"

"I do, damn me to Hell."

She launched herself at him and hugged him, raining kisses on his face. "You love me, Victor! Oh, you and Cabot love me! This will be a happy Christmas." She pulled back, her face shining. "Say it, Victor."

He knew what she needed to hear. What they both needed to hear.

"I love you both," he said.

Cabot moved closer. "Then what do you propose? That we both come to Ralston House and, what, live together without you?"

"I don't think I could bear that," Victor admitted.

"You have but one choice, Victor," Cabot said.

And then he knew. Deep in his soul, he knew. He could have what all those happy Hawks seemed to have found. Two loves to complete him and give him the chance he'd never thought to take.

"Marry me, Violet?" he asked, taking her hands in his. "Be my wife and live at Ralston House with Cabot and me?"

"With Cabot and you?" she asked.

"With Cabot and you?" Cabot asked. "That is, with me as well?"

Victor smiled, a full expression he didn't believe he'd ever worn before. "Yes. Come live with us. Not as my valet and certainly not as a pet."

"Do you mean it?" Cabot asked.

"I do. My wife-to-be is in love with you, Cabot. How could I deny her desires?"

"Wife-to-be," Violet whispered.

"Will you marry me?" he asked her again.

Her eyes turned deep purple as she beamed at him. "I will."

He kissed her and then Cabot, feeling as if a large weight had been lifted off his chest.

As they began to kiss and caress each other, Victor knew this was right. This was his happiness. To hell with his vow. He would make a new one.

Being faithful to his wife and lover wouldn't be a challenge. He truly didn't want any others but them. He vowed instead to be happy for once in his damned life.

And with Violet and Cabot in his life, he would have everything. This he knew with all his heart.

THE END

WWW.JOSIEDENNIS.COM

ABOUT THE AUTHOR

Josie Dennis writes erotic romances for the discerning reader. Her characters find love in the most amazing places, and the Happily Ever After is a guarantee. Readers who like their romances hot and their heroes and heroines open to ideas they've only explored in their fantasies will find her erotic romances quite satisfying.

For all titles by Josie Dennis, please visit
www.bookstrand.com/josie-dennis

Siren Publishing, Inc.
www.SirenPublishing.com

CPSIA information can be obtained at www.ICGtesting.com
Printed in the USA
BVOW05s1413110314

347320BV00009B/116/P